Emmerda
A SAD AND
A S

The truth was, Henry wa
like living alone. And the best arrang
marry Alison Gibbons and take a house somewher
Beckindale to start a new life. After all, he wasn't old. Fifty wasn't old these days. With a wife like Alison, everything could be fresh and young again. Alison was just right – she'd seen a a bit of life, suffered a little, understood that you had to work at being happy.

The problem was to know whether she thought of him as a possible partner now. That former rejection was behind them; it didn't trouble him at all that she had a prison sentence in her past, which was the reason she had given for refusing him. It seemed she was coming back to life in a more complete way than ever before, for now she was positively flirting with several men.

Well, perhaps not flirting. He had to admit she wasn't the flighty sort. But dammit, there were three men after her! That couldn't happen without some sort of encouragement on her part.

Henry was perplexed. He didn't know what to do to come out ahead of the other two. They were so totally different . . .

Also by Lee Mackenzie in *Star*

EMMERDALE FARM: THE LEGACY
EMMERDALE FARM: PRODIGAL'S PROGRESS
EMMERDALE FARM: ALL THAT A MAN HAS . . .
EMMERDALE FARM: LOVERS' MEETING

EMMERDALE FARM BOOK 5

A SAD AND HAPPY SUMMER

Lee Mackenzie

Based on the successful Yorkshire Television series originated by Kevin Laffan

STAR

A STAR BOOK
published by
the Paperback Division of
W. H. ALLEN & Co Ltd

A Star Book
Published in 1978
by the Paperback Division of
W. H. Allen & Co. Ltd
A Howard and Wyndham Company
44 Hill Street, London W1X 8LB
Reprinted in 1978 (three times)

Printed in Great Britain by Cox & Wyman Ltd,
London, Reading and Fakenham

ISBN 0 352 30142 2

CHAPTER ONE

While Joe Sugden was falling in love with Christine Sharp, his brother-in-law Matt was embarking on a love affair – after his own quiet style.

Almost no one at Emmerdale Farm could have said with certainty what Matt Skilbeck was thinking. He was quiet, undemanding. Annie Sugden suspected that he hadn't recovered yet from the death of his wife Peggy, but she couldn't have given chapter and verse for this belief, for Matt never spoke of Peggy unless someone else brought up the subject; but though no one really knew Matt's inner self, Annie perhaps had more insight than most. She wasn't a typical mother-in-law; she had seen faults in Peggy that Matt seemed unaware of, or, if he saw them, forgave. Annie had always thought that her only daughter got a better husband than she perhaps deserved.

To be left a widower, with baby twins to care for, was a catastrophe that would have felled most men. Matt somehow survived with dignity, with what almost looked like tranquillity. When, at last, he felt it was only fair on the community at Emmerdale to let his aunt and uncle take the babies as temporary foster-children, the decision was taken on the grounds that it put too much of a strain on Annie to have to look after them on top of all her work on the farm. It was typical of Matt to put others first. He missed the twins, no doubt of that – but he was firm against Annie's pleas that she could manage.

'Nay, it's not fair,' he told her in a gentle tone. 'It were bad enough when you were fit, but now you've sprained your wrist it's just not on, Ma.'

'We could make arrangements, Matt. We could get someone in to help temporarily—'

'Who, for instance? The Blakeys are leaving for the south so Frank can take up a teaching job, your cousin Beryl's gone after all that trouble about Sharon's death, Mrs Ruskin's got her hands full with all the vicar's committees and meetings ...

Nay, it's best to let the twins stay with Auntie Beattie and Uncle Ben.'

'Alison Gibbons said she'd be glad to come up to Emmerdale—'

'Alison's got a shop to run,' Matt said, rather tersely for him. 'Let be, Ma. I'm not doing this just for a whim. I've thought about it, and I reckon they're better off at Middleton's with Auntie Beattie. After all, she was a trained children's nurse, and they've got a nice cottage there, and Uncle Ben isn't hard pressed with his chauffeuring for Middleton so he can pull his weight with the kiddies . . .'

Taken aback to find he had thought it through so far, Annie had nothing to say. Within herself she regretted the decision: the twins had been so important to her as the one remaining link with wayward, quick-thinking Peggy. Yet there was more to her regret – she felt that after the going of the twins, Matt retired yet further into himself.

She made great efforts to keep close touch with the grandchildren. She seized every opportunity to be driven the fifteen miles across the dale to Middleton's estate for a visit with them, and even got into the habit of using the telephone, that hated instrument, to chat with Auntie Beattie.

'Costs a fortune,' grumbled Old Sam, each time she picked up the receiver. 'Throwing money away, that's what it is.'

'Dad, the telephone was invented so that people could talk to each other!'

'Aye, but why don't you wait till people ring *you*? A lot cheaper that way.'

With something between a laugh and a sigh, Annie ignored him. She had something to discuss with Matt's Auntie Beattie – the christening of the twins.

Little Sam and Sally were well into the crawling stage now, but they still had not been christened. It troubled Annie, who was a staunch churchgoer and, more important, a convinced believer in the Christian faith. She had tiptoed up to the subject with Matt, and withdrawn from it – for Matt was not a believer.

Why should he be? How was it possible to believe in a kind and loving God if He took away a young wife a few weeks after the birth of her children? 'Suffer the little children . . .' Well, they did suffer, indeed they did, if they were deprived of their mother – so Matt told himself in the dark moments of his grief.

Never much of a churchgoer, he turned away completely after Peggy's death. He listened with a quiet, controlled gaze while the vicar tried to comfort and explain, yet Edward Ruskin knew he had failed to help him. The weeks turned into months, and still Matt stayed away from church.

Then one morning Ruskin found him in the graveyard, staring down at his wife's grave. Only the simplest marker denoted Peggy's resting-place; everyone at Emmerdale was waiting for the time – if it ever came – when they could consult with Matt on some wording for a gravestone.

'I was thinking, Vicar,' Matt murmured, staring down at the turf, 'that Peggy would have liked it if there were a tree growing over her . . .'

'Why – yes, she would!' Ruskin said, carefully disguising his eagerness. Mustn't frighten him off! This was a first step towards letting Peggy become a less painful memory. 'What kind of tree? Did you have anything in mind?'

Matt hesitated. 'Up to you, isn't it? The land here belongs to t'church.'

'Oh, but in the case of memorial plants—'

'Aye, but you wouldn't want an oak growing here and breaking up t'old gravestones wi' its roots, now would you?'

'Hardly,' Ruskin agreed with a smile. 'But an oak wouldn't be right for Peggy.'

'No-o . . .' A pause. 'I were thinking of a flowering tree . . .'

'Yes, something light and graceful.'

'Aye, the way she was when she was alive.' Matt bit his lip. After a moment he went on, 'I thought mebbe a may tree. Or a cherry.'

'Yes, beautiful. I think either would be beautiful.'

'Right.' A sigh. 'I'll go into Ditchling's Nurseries and take a look.'

'Take your time.'

'I'd like to choose it soon. It ought to go in during t'winter, when it's dormant, then it can get a good start when spring comes.'

'That's true.'

'Aye, then I'll go next weekend. Thank you, Vicar. I'm glad you agree.'

Ruskin stood watching him trudge out of the churchyard. Glad you agree ... The vicar would have agreed to almost anything except a witches' sabbath if it would help Matt Skilbeck express the hidden grief that ate at him.

The slender sapling was planted quietly and without fuss, as Matt did everything. He simply turned up one day, a cold grey December afternoon, with a spade and the little tree wrapped in sacking. Alone – alone as he so often was – Matt dug a careful hole for the roots, cut the string holding the hessian round the root system, spread them carefully in the cavity, and with gentle movements returned the soil. He trod the soil down, tied the sapling to the support he had driven in, and stood back.

'There,' he said, but not aloud. 'I thought you'd like it, Peg.'

His mother-in-law recognized this for a step forward when she saw the little tree. It raised hopes within her that perhaps in the not too distant future she could speak to him about the christening of the babies. But Christmas was just coming – Christmas, the time of children, with its bitter-sweet memories of other times when Peggy had been there ordering everyone about in her bright, brisk way. Christmas was too hurtful a time to talk about such a delicate matter.

The bitter winter weather held the land in a grip of iron for the first few days of January. The January sales were on in the big towns, so Alison Gibbons proposed to Annie that they should have a jaunt to Leeds to look for bargains. 'Do come, Annie! I want to buy material for a dress and I need an opinion—'

'Nay, you know more about fashion than I do, Alison,' Annie returned, eyeing the display of new frozen foods in the village shop as she spoke. 'Got a big bag of peas?'

'A freezer pack? They're coming in tomorrow.'

'But I shan't be coming into Beckindale tomorrow.'

'Tell you what,' Alison said, turning her mischievous smile on Annie, 'I'll bring the peas up to Emmerdale tomorrow if you'll come on from there with me to Leeds for a sales spree – how about that?'

Despite herself, Annie laughed. 'You're a shrewd negotiator, Alison.'

'Have to be, haven't I? Running a village shop is like high finance, only on a small scale. *Quid pro quo*, I think it's called!'

She leaned on the counter and tilted her head. 'Don't you think it would do you good to get out for an afternoon, Annie? You worked hard at Christmas, and now you've got all this bother with the men putting in the milk tank and Joe up all hours of the day and night taking milk records and so on . . . I always think it does anybody good to have a bit of a cheer-up in January, anyway.'

'Nowt wrong with January,' Annie objected. 'Part of the year, like seedtime and harvest—'

'But not nearly so much fun! Now admit it, Annie – January's the time when everything goes dead. Let's go out and live a little.'

'By choosing dress material?'

'Oh, we might even have a cup of tea and a squishy cake in a café!' Alison giggled. 'If we arrange things nicely, we might delay our trip home until after the pubs are open in which case I'll stand you a sherry in a genteel saloon bar.'

Annie sensed that Alison herself was in need of a little fillip to her morale. After all, it couldn't be exactly lively to be part owner and sole salesgirl in a tiny village shop in the Dales, especially to a woman like Alison who had been used to big town life. She seemed to enjoy Beckindale and all its activities, yet it was always something of a puzzle to Annie why someone as attractive and lively should bury herself here. Alison had been born in Liverpool, that much she knew; and there had been a husband, of whom Alison hardly ever spoke. Beyond that, although she liked her, Annie knew nothing.

It was only reasonable that she should sometimes want a little amusement beyond what the village had to offer. 'All right,' Annie agreed, 'it's a deal. You deliver my freezer pack of peas, and I'll go with you to Leeds tomorrow afternoon.'

They had an enjoyable outing. To her own surprise, Annie found one or two things she wanted to buy – knitting wool, for instance, really seemed to have been reduced considerably so she bought twenty-four ounces to make suits for the twins. She looked at the new cleaners – it would be rather nice to have something a bit more modern than the heavy old vacuum she pulled round the house.

Alison bought material after much comparing and considering. 'I really like the blue,' she mused, 'but I'd made up my mind to have something more neutral . . .'

'The blue's a real bargain,' Annie said, nipping it between finger and thumb. 'It's pure wool.'

'Yes, but I've got brown and tan sweaters . . . And an over-dress in blue isn't really right to wear with those . . . Oh, I've got to make a choice so I'll have the beige!'

That done, they had the cup of tea that Alison had promised, and indeed the squishy cakes. Then they went for a last wander before heading for the bus station. 'I would rather like a blouse,' Alison murmured.

'Oh, we should have looked while we were in the store, Alison. We passed the separates department.'

'No, I would really like something more delicate, Annie. You know? The old-fashioned kind with tucks and lace – to wear in the evenings.'

'Oh yes, I know. Well, there's the boutiques in the arcade.'

'Oh, they're full of tat from Afghanistan and places like that. No, I don't mean tat – they're all right, those things, but you know the colour runs hideous when you wash them . . . And besides I don't want something foreign. You know the kind of thing that used to be handmade in crèpe de chine, Annie?'

'Some hopes,' Annie said. 'Nobody makes that kind of thing any more.' She paused. 'Although . . . there used to be a shop in Deacon Row . . .'

'Deacon Row? Where's that?'

'Not far. Come on, we'll take a look.'

The shop was a hang-over from times gone by, what used to be called a linen-shop. It sold embroidered tea-cloths, lace bed-spreads, doylies, and antimacassars. But it also stocked baby-wear and blouses – not handmade in crèpe de chine, but of a kind different from the goods available in department stores.

Alison was soon happy looking at the selection of frilled, tucked and lace-trimmed blouses. Annie meanwhile wandered to the other side where the babywear was on show. There was a pretty little linen smock decorated with yellow ducks – just right for little Sally in three or four months time when the good weather came. And a sort of modernized sailor-suit that would look a treat on Sam. But oh, the prices.

She was attracted further on by a 'Sale' sign. 'Greatly reduced, Cannot be repeated,' it announced. She went up to look at the stand.

Christening robes.

It almost seemed like a sign from heaven. Annie had a christening robe put away, the one that had been used successively for Jack, Peggy and Joe and before that for Annie herself and her sisters. But if the twins were to be christened, they would need two christening robes. She had been thinking for quite a while that she ought to inquire in the family for a second gown, or begin making one; and yet it seemed pointless if Matt were going to remain adamant about not having Sam and Sally baptized.

As she ran her finger along the scalloped edge of the cambric gown, she thought how lovely it would be to have Sally in her arms, wearing this, in the church where her own children had been christened. She ought to speak to Matt: to have seen this gown was a reminder to her that this important duty had not yet been carried out. She wasn't one to believe in messages from the Almighty as a rule, but all the same – to walk into the shop looking for a fashion blouse and find just the robe for little Sally! It was too much of a coincidence.

She chose her moment with care, later that evening. Joe had gone to a meeting in Hotten about the Urban District Council's plans for weed control of the hedgerows, Sam had been taken to an indoor bowls match by an old crony. The kitchen at Emmerdale was warm and cosy with the fire gleaming behind its bars, the soft light reflected on Annie's copper pans. Annie knitted in silence for some moments.

'Alison and I had a really nice afternoon,' she began. She had noticed before now that Matt liked to hear news of Alison.

'Aye, you've got started on the suits for the twins already, I see.'

'Have to, or the spring'll be here and thick wool like this would be too warm.' She finished the row and counted her stitches. 'I saw something else that would have been just right for them,' she added.

'Oh? What was that?'

'A real bargain. Reduced to half price.'

'Well, what?' Matt asked lazily, stretching out his legs

towards the fire. 'I'd like 'em to have anything they need, Annie. You know that.'

'The problem is, *I* think it would be something they need – only I don't know if you'll agree.'

Matt sat up straight. He had guessed that this wasn't a casual conversation after all. 'What do the twins need, Annie?'

'They need christening robes, Matt.'

'Oh.' His broad face went very still. 'I thought I'd explained how I feel about that, Annie.'

'Yes, you did, Matt. And I respect your feelings. I'm just wondering if you're going to go on feeling the same for ever? I hope the time will come when you'll change your mind and agree to have them named in church, like Peggy was, and like she'd have wanted if she'd lived.'

'But she didn't live, did she?' His voice was low. 'That's the point, isn't it? Whatever Peggy might have wanted, she isn't here to see to it.'

'But that isn't a reason to keep from carrying out her wishes, Matt. Not as I see it.'

'There was no reason for taking away her life either, Ma. She couldn't have "wished" to be taken from Sam and Sally. To my mind, her wishes have been set aside by someone stronger than us – and I don't want to argue about that because I know you don't agree with me.'

'Matt, I wouldn't want to distress you,' Annie said. 'I'm only reminding you that Sam and Sally have rights too—'

'What?' The blond head jerked up as he turned from gazing into the fire. 'Are you saying I'm denying something to Sam and Sally?'

'Well, aren't you?'

He got to his feet. Slowly he went to the hooks by the door and took down his coat. 'I think I'll go to the Woolpack for a drink,' he said.

'Nay, don't go, son!' she cried. 'Don't make me feel I've driven you from your own fireside—'

'It's all right, Ma. There's got to be times when we don't see eye to eye.' His tone implied, 'Even you and I can disagree.'

When he had gone, she continued with her knitting for a while. Then, setting it by, she went up to her own room. There she opened the wardrobe and took from the recesses a shallow cardboard box, which she opened. Inside, within layers of tissue paper, lay the gown of fine lawn and crocheted lace that had been worn by her children at their baptism. She ran her hand over it, feeling the worn forefinger of her right hand catch on the lace. After a moment, with a shake of the head, she put the lid back on the box and took it back to the wardrobe.

Not yet. She had been too precipitate. She might have known, she said to herself with a wry smile, that the Almighty was not addressing any special messages to Annie Sugden in a linen-shop in Leeds. She only hoped she hadn't done any damage by rushing in where angels feared to tread.

Nevertheless the Almighty might have been giving a little attention to Emmerdale after all, for the matter didn't rest there. Alison Gibbons came to the farm a few days later to ask Annie to pin the hem on the new beige overdress, and after a session in Annie's bedroom with pins and chalk she was asked to stay for a cup of tea.

'You know what I wish?' she queried as she sipped. 'I wish I'd bought the blue.'

'Blue what?' asked Joe Sugden, offering her a biscuit.

'The blue material that I saw last Saturday when I went to Leeds with your mother.'

'Don't you like that biscuity colour?'

'Oh yes, I love it. I wish I'd bought the blue as well.'

Joe grinned at Matt. 'There's feminine logic for you. Goes to the sales to save money, and then wishes she'd spent more than she already has.'

'But it was such a bargain,' Alison insisted. 'Pure wool.'

'I told you at the time, Alison.'

'I know. I should have bought it.'

'Well, go back and get it.'

Alison sighed. 'Can't get away till next Saturday afternoon. And the bus is always so full on Saturday.'

'Hey,' said Joe, 'one of us ought to go into Leeds to buy that book about weed control by spraying.'

'We can get it by post,' Matt said, practical as ever.

'Oh, get on! It's more fun to go into Leeds than send a cheque for it.'

'All right then, you go.'

'All right then, I will! And I'll give you a lift in, Alison.'

'Oh, thank you, that's great Joe.' Alison's grey eyes were sparkling at the thought. 'I'll get enough for a dress and jacket – that way I can wear it right through into April, and then I can wear just the dress—'

'Spare us the details,' Joe said. 'We're too dense to understand mix'n'match, or whatever you call it.'

'I see you know the term, anyhow. Which one of your girlfriends talks to you about fashion?'

'The ones who can get a word in edgeways,' Matt teased. 'But hang on a bit – weren't you to go to Harrogate on Saturday to collect entry forms for the Great Yorkshire Show?'

'Oh heck. So I was. Well, I'll leave that till next week. It's not urgent. The show isn't until August.'

'I want to know about the entry qualifications for the new categories, Joe.'

'Well, you go to Harrogate, then.'

'Nay, we don't want both to be away from t'farm.'

'Nonsense. As long as we see to milking, that's all that's needed – we don't both have to be here.'

'If I'm going out for the afternoon, I'd rather go to Leeds than Harrogate. There's a piece I need for the tractor engine that I could get at that secondhand dealer in Leeds.'

'All right then,' Joe cried. 'You go to Leeds and I'll go to Harrogate. There you are, Alison – you don't mind having poor old Matt instead of handsome young Joe, do you?'

'Now, now, that's no way to talk, Joe,' his mother reproved.

'I think I can put up with it,' Alison said with a mischievous glint. 'Although, as a matter of fact, you remind me of a film star who was called Joe.'

'Really?' Joe said, falling into the trap. 'Who's that?'

'Mighty Joe Young.'

'Oh aye, I've heard of him.'

'Is it a date then, Matt?' Alison went on. 'Are we going to Leeds on Saturday?'

'Aye,' Matt said, rather shy, 'if you want to.'

'I certainly do. Will you pick me up?'

'Half-one?'

'Right. Thanks for the tea, Annie.' Alison went to the door and opened it.

'Hi,' Joe said just as she stepped out, 'weren't Mighty Joe Young a gorilla or summat?'

'I *told* you you reminded me of him,' Alison called as she departed.

'Cheeky thing,' Joe laughed.

'But she's never unkind with it,' Matt put in.

'Nay, she's a nice lass, is Alison,' Annie agreed. 'Couldn't meet a nicer.'

Matt was in complete agreement. The thought of spending an afternoon with Alison was very pleasurable to him. It would be the first time he had gone shopping with a woman since Peggy died, if you excepted some little excursions with his mother-in-law. He would have winced away from it if it had been anyone else – no joshing or teasing by Joe could have chivvied him into it if it had been a woman other than Alison.

Sometimes he felt drawn to her. He sensed, behind the bright determination of her manner and the bravery of her solitary life, a loneliness that was akin to his own She was a widow; what kind of husband had she had? What kind of marriage?

He wouldn't have dreamed of putting such questions to her. But it so happened that she gave him some of the answers during Saturday.

They got to Leeds very early. Instead of plunging straight into the shopping expedition, they went for a walk near the university. The students were still on Christmas holiday but one or two were about, strolling in conversation with books under their arms.

'Must be funny, having nothing else to do but read books,' Matt remarked.

'It's a thing you've never thought of trying, I take it.'

'Not me!' he laughed. 'I'm no scholar. Can't imagine what it would be like, working with my head instead of my hands.'

'Oh, you can't breed championship ewes without using brains, Matt!'

He considered that. 'But it isn't book-learning. I couldn't learn things out of a book. I expect it makes you a more interesting person if you can.'

'Interesting? Ye-es . . .' She paused. 'My husband was a graduate.'

'Was he?' Matt was startled at mention of him. He couldn't

recall Alison ever bringing him into a conversation before. 'Here in Leeds?'

'No, he was a Liverpool man. That was how I came to meet him – he was back home after completing a post-graduate course at Harvard. It made him seem very ... glamorous. To have been to America, I mean.'

'Yes,' Matt agreed. 'That's a long way to go for education, isn't it?'

She smiled to herself. 'That was typical of Peter – he'd go anywhere in furtherance of his career.'

'He did well, I suppose?'

'No, he didn't.' She sighed. 'He was a strange mixture, my husband. Full of ambition, and yet he didn't have the determination ... And sometimes he ... he could be very ... very thoughtless.'

Matt took her arm to help her over some slippery stones where the ice hadn't melted in the puddles. 'But you were happy,' he suggested.

'Yes. No. I don't know.' She held on fast to his arm. 'I don't think I was, really. But it broke me in two when he died.'

Matt was afraid to carry on the conversation. Her voice was strange – sharp with pain and remembered misery. They walked in silence for a time.

'I'm sorry,' she said all at once. 'I didn't mean to go on like that. It's just that you brought it to my mind when you talked about working with your head. Peter used to say that – "You've got to use your head." I came to recognize it as an excuse when he wanted to do something that his heart should have rebelled against.'

'That's sad, Alison. I'm sorry.'

She hugged his arm. 'Come on, that's enough of that. Let's go to the shops. I'll take you to a lovely little place that Annie and I went to last Saturday. She nearly bought a christening robe for one of your twins.'

To her surprise she felt him stiffen and stop. She turned to him in question. 'What's the matter?'

'I don't want to go to a shop where they sell christening robes.'

She would have laughed, at the incongruous words on his

masculine lips, except that he was so clearly serious. 'No, I suppose it's not your kind of shopping.'

'I didn't mean that. I've told Annie already – I'm not having the twins christened.'

She drew in a sharp breath. 'Forgive me for barging in. Only Annie was so interested in the robes—'

'She's keen on that kind of thing.'

'But you're not?'

'I'm not much of a churchgoer.'

She hesitated. 'Neither am I. But I think I go along with having babies christened. It may be a convention, but there's something . . . reassuring about it.'

'But there's something dishonest about going through with a thing just because it's a convention, Alison—'

'Isn't there something rather selfish about going against a convention just because you want your own way?'

'Oh, I don't think I—'

'I'm thinking about myself, not you, Matt. I went against the conventions when I first met Peter. I wanted to live with him – not married, you know, just living together. I had a view of life then – I thought it was revolutionary and liberated, but I see now that it was just trendy and selfish.'

'You're hard on yourself.'

'Not as hard as I should have been then. I made a lot of people very unhappy just for a point of view that I hadn't really examined.'

'And what happened?'

'In the end I got married. I did it to please my mother, or so I thought. I look back now and I see that I was quite content to fall in with convention when it came to the nitty-gritty. I didn't inflict humiliation and gossip on my mother and in the long run I saw that I had been clinging to a sham integrity—'

'I see what you're trying to say, Alison,' Matt interrupted. 'But this business of being christened isn't the same. It doesn't make any difference to kids – nobody ever asks them afterwards or, if they do, they don't hold it against them when the answer's no. The way I see it, it doesn't matter, and I don't fancy putting my kids through a ceremony that I don't set any store by.'

'But other people do, Matt.'

'You mean Annie.'

'And your uncle and aunt, surely.'

'Yes, them too. And grandad. Grandad is upset about it, I can see that whenever the point comes up.'

'It doesn't occur to you,' Alison said carefully, 'that you may be wrong when so many people you respect are against you?'

He sighed deeply. 'Of course it occurs to me. I've had this argument with myself time and again.'

'I see.'

'Happen I ought to have it again, though,' he said with glum humour. 'You've shaken my faith in my own rightness.'

It was a conversation he wouldn't have dreamed of having with anyone else, not even with Annie. He shied away from talking about deep things but something in Alison seemed to call forth a stream of articulate expression he hadn't known himself capable of. When he thought it over afterwards he was astonished, and yet he was pleased. It was comforting to know he could be in touch with someone else's inner thoughts and give his own in exchange, without being clumsy or embarrassed.

When Matt announced a few days later that he had decided to have his babies christened, Annie was surprised but delighted. She couldn't imagine what had occurred to change his mind. Alison too was pleased; she had a feeling that something she had said might have influenced him, and that was rather a flattering thought.

As she spent a winter evening stacking new goods on the shelves of her shop, it occurred to her that it would be only too fatally easy to get fond of Matt Skilbeck.

CHAPTER TWO

Henry Wilks hadn't failed to notice the growing friendship between Alison and Matt. It was a matter that was bound to concern him, for Henry had once proposed to Alison and been refused on grounds he considered quite inadequate. He still hoped to capture her in the end, and he didn't want Matt Skilbeck getting in the way. Matt was a good chap, none better – but he didn't think he was right for Alison.

He was even more perturbed when Matt asked Alison to be a godmother to little Sally. That seemed to imply a relationship between them that was more important than Henry had bargained for. After all, you don't ask just anyone to act godparent to your children.

Henry of course was unaware of the conversation the two of them had had, the conversation which had played so big a part in bringing Matt to his decision. All he knew was that he, Henry, had only stepped in as a godfather when Jack Sugden failed to turn up from Rome, which seemed to mean that he, Henry, was a sort of second-best choice whereas Alison had been a first-line godparent. It troubled him.

He found himself taking every excuse for going into the shop to talk to Alison. There was always some good reason; as her partner in the business he had a right to be there, and he could always plead his financial expertise when he popped in to offer advice. They had had a long conversation at the end of January and decided, after the crush Alison had experienced in the big shops on Saturday, that from February onwards she should close the village shop on Wednesday so that she could have an easier time if she went into town on her day off.

He went into the shop the Wednesday after the christening, to remind her – as if she needed reminding.

'Oh, I've got this afternoon all planned,' she told him. 'It's like being let out of a cage.'

'I thought you liked running the shop,' he said, shocked.

'I do,' she assured him. 'But I used to like school, and yet I still felt marvellous when playtime came round.'

'Oh . . . I see . . .' He was greatly relieved. The fact was that Henry had only put up the other half of the money to help Alison to buy the shop lease so as to keep her in Beckindale. He had no great interest in groceries or general merchandise. Oh, of course, he was pleased to help keep the shop going as a service to the people of the district, but he wouldn't have bothered unduly if Alison hadn't expressed an interest in it as a livelihood.

'Remember when we used to go bird-watching?' he said.

Alison wasn't likely to forget it. They had found the shoe of poor Sharon Crossthwaite once when they were out bird-watching, and had carefully set it on a boulder for its owner to find, quite unaware that Sharon's body was lying in the ruins of the old abbey nearby.

'I'm thinking of going out this afternoon,' Henry went on, unaware of the shiver his first words had brought to her. 'Care to join me?'

'Oh . . . No, sorry, Henry . . . I've got other arrangements.'

'Anything important? Perhaps you could change them.'

'Er . . . No, Henry, I think I'd rather just leave them the way they are.'

'Oh . . . Some other time, then?'

'Some other time, I'd love to.'

'I'll hold you to that.' Defeated, he went to the Woolpack (where he had a reasonably comfortable room and a share in the proceeds) lunched on a pork pie and a glass of ale, and went out to watch the birds of February on his own.

That was how he came to see Alison with Matt Skilbeck, down by the river in the cold afternoon light, flicking the water in hopes of catching a grayling or two with a rather fine split cane rod.

It was Alison's first fishing lesson. 'I've never seen you here fishing,' she remarked to Matt.

'Don't have much time. I used to come once – Peg was quite keen. This is her rod, really. I gave it to her for her birthday the first year I knew her.'

She knew at once that it was an honour to be allowed to handle the rod, and at once became stiff and self-conscious.

'Nay,' Matt protested, 'you'll never be able to cast if you don't let your wrist go. Like this.' He put an arm about her to show her how to turn her shoulder away and free her arm and wrist for the forward movement.

Henry, watching them from the woods on the crest of the valley, felt a twinge of anxiety. He understood that Matt was only giving instruction on how to handle the rod . . . Yet all the same, Matt was there, with Alison, putting his arm about her without any protest from her; whereas when Henry invited her out, she had put him off quite calmly.

He didn't know whether to be glad or sorry when yet a third claimant appeared on the scene. This was Dryden Hogben, who took everyone by surprise by turning up with a little tent and a few billycans to camp in the wilderness that had once been the garden of Henry's burnt-out house.

Dryden – or Dry, as he liked to be called – was a strange bundle of contradictions. He was big and tall and agile, yet he was no youngster. As Joe Sugden pointed out, most of the folk who turned up with a pup tent and a sleeping-bag were students, seeing the country the cheap way.

Dry was different. He seemed to have no desire to move on, and wasn't heading anywhere in particular. Henry thought he was about thirty. That didn't matter much, except that he was handsome – tousled dark hair, fine beard framing a square jaw, keen dark eyes and a flashing smile. As if that wasn't enough, there was this air of mystery that surrounded him. He had no money – not just very little money, absolutely *no* money.

'You could get some from Social Security, couldn't you?' Henry suggested, practical as ever.

'Could you?'

'Of course you could.'

'You need to have a settled address before you can claim Social Security,' Alison put in.

'My goodness, what a lot you know,' Dry said in admiration.

'You have a settled address, don't you?'

'Yes, Henry's garden,' Dry said.

'No, I mean a real settled address. You belong somewhere.'

'I don't believe I do.'

'But you have relatives? Friends?'

'How much are baked beans?' Dry inquired. 'Mrs Sugden paid me twenty pence for finding her apron when it flew off the wash line.'

'Twenty pence?' Henry exclaimed. 'Surely Annie would never offer a man twenty pence!'

'Oh, she offered me more, but I told her it was only worth twenty pence. Don't you think that was fair? I only had to cross one field to get it.'

'But, good Lord—!'

'Look, if I had been a little boy she'd have given me a five-penny piece. It's only because I'm a grown man that she tried to hand out fifty pence. That's taking advantage of age discrimination, in my view.'

'Age discrimination? What the devil's that?' Henry cried, baffled.

'Oh, it's what makes people advertise jobs in the papers and say "Not over forty" or what makes it impossible for me to tell you to drop dead when you try to get me to go to the Social Security Department.'

Henry's mouth fell open. Alison dissolved into giggles and had to hold on to the shop counter for support.

'How much are baked beans?' Dry resumed, pointing.

Pulling herself together, Alison fetched the tin. As she gave him change she said, 'What is it that prevents you from telling me to drop dead when I try to find out where you hail from?'

He grinned. 'The fact that you're prettier than Henry,' he said, and went out.

Henry at last found his voice as the tinkle of the shop doorbell faded. 'Well, the impertinent rascal—'

'You must admit we asked for it, Henry.'

'Nothing of the kind. I was trying to do him a good turn.'

'He's the kind of man who prefers not to be patronized, I think.'

'Dammit, I wasn't patronizing him—'

'Weren't you, Henry? I felt you were. Just as I felt I was being nosy, when I stopped to think about it.'

'But you didn't think he was cheeky when he answered you back.'

'No. In fact, I thought he was rather nice to me. I like the man.'

Henry tweaked his neat little moustache and buttoned up his expensive sheepskin coat. 'I'm off,' he said. 'I only dropped in to remind you of your promise to come birdwatching some time.'

'Oh, Henry, it's too cold for birdwatching.'

He was disappointed. 'Well then ... come out for a meal with me.'

'All right.'

'All right?' He was taken aback.

'All right. You asked me out for a meal, I'm accepting.'

'Well ... well ... That's marvellous!' Henry was lost between delight and surprise. He had never expected an acceptance of his invitation, because somehow he'd taken it for granted that he would be taking a back seat to such glamorous 'Outsider' figures as Dry Hogben, never mind the sturdy yeoman appearance of Matt Skilbeck. 'Well, what evening shall we say? Tonight? Tomorrow?'

'Not tonight, Henry. As it's my half-day I've got things planned already—'

'With Matt?' Henry demanded, unable to prevent himself.

Alison's grey eyes surveyed him with calm interest. 'Yes, as a matter of fact, with Matt. He's teaching me how to fish.'

'Oh. Well. Yes, I knew that, as a matter of fact.'

'Did you now?'

'Happened to see you the other day ...'

'Mm ... m ...' She turned and began to put packets of custard powder upright where they had fallen over on the shelf. 'You and half of Beckindale, I imagine.'

'It isn't a secret, is it?'

'No hopes of that, in a place like this.'

'Did you want it to be a secret?'

'No,' she said after a moment's thought, 'but I don't want it to be a subject of conversation either.'

'That's not reasonable, Alison. Of course folks are interested in what other folk do.'

'I agree. It's the things they read into it that bother me.'

'How d'you mean, read into it?'

'Matt is teaching me how to fish. That's it. Nothing more. Do you think everyone in Beckindale accepts that?'

All at once Henry felt much better. 'About our date. How about Friday night?'

'Not Friday. I'm doing something Friday.'

'Saturday then.'

'All right. Saturday.'

'Pick you up here?'

'Thank you.'

'I know just the place,' he enthused. 'Doesn't look up to much but the food's great.'

'I'll look forward to that, then.'

'Six o'clock?'

'Yes, I'll be ready.'

Much comforted, Henry pulled up the collar of his sheepskin coat and braved the elements for a walk to Emmerdale, where a meeting of the farm management committee was due. He would have been less pleased with life had he known that the reason Alison couldn't accept his invitation for Friday was that she had agreed to go out for a meal on that evening with Matt.

Emmerdale Farm Limited held regular meetings to plan their programme of crops and activities. The big item this time was Joe's plan to get the herd certificated as free of tuberculosis, which meant a big investment of time and money in fencing and walling – for if a non-certificated animal wandered in, the herd could be contaminated.

Henry was in favour of this, in principle, but wondered whether they had enough staff to undertake the work. 'Would we have to hire extra?' he asked. 'On day wages?'

'We could manage,' Matt said.

'And we've got Christine helping us for the moment,' Joe put in.

Christine Sharp was the girl who had come from the Milk Marketing Board to offer advice on Low Cost Production techniques, during the autumn of the previous year. Slender, dark and fragile-looking, she had now thrown herself into the hard labour of running Emmerdale as some repayment for Annie's kindness in offering her bed and board. Henry didn't quite understand the ins and outs of her stay at the farm. When he asked Annie, she murmured, 'Oh, some trouble with her dad, I think. It'll work itself out, Henry.'

Now Henry said, 'Are we paying her wages?'

'We-ell . . . no.'

'If she's to be counted as part of the farm staff, oughtn't we to be paying her?'

'Henry's got a point,' Matt said. 'Labourer's worthy of his hire, as the saying goes.'

'Aye. But what hire? What kind of wages do we offer her?'

'It wants thinking on,' Joe said, colouring a little. 'I don't know how she'd feel about being offered money.'

'Now come on, Joe. If a girl is employed by us, she's got to be paid. What would it look like in the accounts at the end of the financial year?'

'I don't know that she's exactly employed by us. More a volunteer, like.'

'You mean, student helper? Something like that?'

'We'll talk to Christine about it,' Annie promised.

'Can't we have her in now and talk to her?'

'Nay,' Joe said quickly, 'leave it with us, Henry. She's ... she's in a bit of an emotional state. Might just take off if we started talking money. She says her dad goes on too much about money.'

'What is this, a farm or a psychiatric unit?' Henry grumbled, but in a tone too low to reach Joe. Louder he said, 'Well, leave that then. Next item?'

'Landrover's playing up again, Henry.'

'Oh no.' He groaned. 'I thought you'd had it fixed?'

'Seems not. Condenser's gone again.'

'Same fault?'

'I reckon.'

'We didn't give 'em enough time last time,' Joe sighed. 'We needed it back in use so we told 'em to get it going. We didn't let them carry out a proper investigation.'

'Right. Then it goes in again and we let Furnival see to it properly.'

'Aye, that's what's needed,' Matt agreed.

'Right. Noted that the Landrover's going in for repair of the fault that's making it unreliable. Next item?'

'Next item is what we're going to use for transport while Landrover's away.'

'It'll only be a few days. A week. That right, Matt?'

'I s'pose so.'

'Then surely we can manage for a week? I mean, I've got a car, and there's the tractor for heavy work.'

'Oh, we'll be all right,' Joe added. 'Christine's got a car too. We'll manage, no problem.'

Matt didn't like to say that he had been relying on the Land-rover to take him and Alison into Hotten on Friday evening. There was a bus service, of course, but the last bus back was at eight o'clock. That didn't allow very long for an evening meal with a lady . . .

Still, he might be able to borrow Henry's car for Friday. He'd ask him when he got him alone for a moment.

The moment didn't come that day. Henry instead chose to walk with Annie to Beckindale, so as to learn a bit more about this girl Christine who seemed to rouse Joe's protective instincts. 'You don't want to worry about that,' she told him. 'Her dad came to see me – right ready for a scrap, he was. But like most folk, his bark's worse than his bite.'

'Sharp, that's the name, isn't it? Seems to me I've heard it. He's in textiles.'

'That's right.'

'A warm man, Annie. Got influence. What did he say about his daughter playing goose-girl at Emmerdale?'

'He said she ought to come home. It's what most fathers would say. But I persuaded him to leave her be for a while so she could get back on an even keel. They've had a row, that's clear. I don't know the rights and wrongs of it, and I don't want to.' Annie sighed. 'I've seen rows between parent and child, Henry. It's my belief that most of them would die away if both sides could just have a cooling off period.'

Henry in his turn gave a sigh. He was thinking of his own daughter, Marian, who had left home in a storm of emotion a year ago and never yet come back. Yet that was not Henry's fault; he had been – he felt – a good and understanding father when she was in the throes of falling in love with Annie's elder son Jack. His fault or no, he had been left lonely and solitary by Marian's departure. He felt he could give Christine's father a warning from his own experience – that young girls were easily upset and needed careful handling.

The truth was, Henry wanted to be married again. He didn't like living alone. After his house was burned down he had eventually settled in at the Woolpack with Amos Brearley, the landlord; he regarded this, however, as a temporary measure. Some day, somehow, he would make some better arrangement.

And the best arrangement of all would be to marry Alison Gibbons and take a house somewhere in Beckindale to start a new life. After all, he wasn't old. Fifty wasn't old these days. With a wife like Alison, everything could be fresh and young again. Alison was just right – she'd seen a bit of life, suffered a little, understood that you had to work at being happy.

The problem was to know whether she thought of him as a possible partner now. That former rejection was behind them; it didn't trouble him at all that she had a prison sentence in her past, which was the reason she had given for refusing him. It seemed she was coming back to life in a more complete way than ever before, for now she was positively flirting with several men.

Well, perhaps not flirting. He had to admit she wasn't the flighty sort. But dammit, there were three men after her! That couldn't happen without some sort of encouragement on her part.

Henry was perplexed. He didn't know what to do to come out ahead of the other two. They were so totally different . . .

One of the suitors consulted Alison about the transport problem on the following day. 'The Landrover's gone into Furnival's for repair,' Matt told her mournfully. 'It means we haven't got a car for tomorrow night.'

'Oh dear. That's a nuisance. The bus comes back so early.'

'Yes, eight o'clock.'

Alison didn't have to say that she thought eight o'clock rather early to conclude a night out. She waited for Matt's views.

'I suppose you don't know what Henry's doing tomorrow night?' he inquired, taking her completely by surprise.

'Henry?'

'I thought, if he wasn't using his car, he might lend it to me.'

With a great effort, she managed not to let him see how the idea perturbed her. 'Er . . . he'd want to know why you want it.'

'I'd tell him – to get to Hotten and back.'

'But he'd ask why you were going to Hotten. It would be only natural.'

'None of his business,' Matt said, although without rancour. 'Still, if he asks me, I'll tell him I'm taking you out.'

'Oh.'

Her tone alerted him. 'You mean you don't want him to know?'

She knew she must be careful how she expressed her thoughts on the matter. 'You see, Matt . . . You've never taken me out to dinner before . . .'

'I know that. What's that matter?'

'It's just that . . . well, you don't seem to be aware that . . . well, people interpret actions in a way that . . . I mean, people talk.'

'Oh aye,' Matt agreed, with a shrug. 'I never understand why they waste their time.'

'But that's *you*, Matt. I've never heard you say an unkind word about anyone. Other people are different. And you know people may be saying things about . . . well, they don't understand it's just fishing lessons.'

'Huh!' Matt thought about it. 'Well, they're right, in a way. It's an evening out now.'

'But you see, Henry . . .'

'You mean Henry's been listening to talk?'

'Yes. No. He didn't need to listen, he saw our fishing expedition.'

'So what, Alison?' And then, almost at once, 'Just a minute. I remember our Jack saying once . . . that Henry was sweet on you at one time.'

She looked down.

'Is that it? He had a fancy for you, happen still has . . .' Matt tried to see this from his own gentle viewpoint. 'Would that stop him from lending me his car?'

'No,' she said, 'I don't think it would stop him. Henry isn't like that. But don't you think it's asking rather a lot of him – really more than just the loan of his car?'

'A lot?' He considered it. 'I see. Yes, it would be a lot to ask. It might hurt him.' He glanced at her. 'You still feel fond of him?'

She had thought he had not sufficient perception to understand that. Like many people, she kept on underestimating Matt.

To break the thread of concentration that had brought them thus far, she began rearranging a counter display of quick-cook pasta. 'This conversation's going in quite the wrong direction,' she said in a too-bright tone.

'No, listen, Alison,' Matt said, refusing to be baulked. 'It's important. Is there something between you and Henry?'

There was no way out. She said, choosing her words with care, 'Henry and I have never been more than friends. We're business partners now too. There was a time when he wanted more than that, but nothing came of it.'

'Because of the way *you* felt? Not from Henry's choice?'

'I suppose you could say that,' she confessed. 'But I thought it was all in the past. It's only recently that . . . that I've suspected Henry still feels something. That being so, I don't want to see him hurt.'

Mercifully at that moment Mrs Bainbridge's daughter came flouncing in for the family's bread. Moments went by while the sliced loaves were loaded into her basket. 'Ta-ra,' she said, and banged the door as she went out.

For a moment after her departure there was a silence.

'I won't ask Henry for the car,' Matt said.

She smiled her gratitude.

'I'll just have to think of something else.' He went to the door with a pensive tilt to his head. Once there, he paused with his hand on the knob. 'You *will* still come?'

'Even if we have to walk to Hotten and back,' she said.

As Matt walked back to Emmerdale he felt he had been given a big, unexpected present.

Alison hoped that she'd handled things right. She had little experience of keeping up a friendship with two men at the same time, and it didn't occur to her to play one off against the other. She found it a difficult situation, chiefly because she liked them both.

She had no idea that she was about to be given a third suitor, one that she hadn't expected. He walked into the Woolpack at lunchtime while she was having a sherry in the short interval during which she closed the village shop.

'Morning,' he said.

'Good morning, Dry.'

'Morning, Amos.'

Amos Brearley muttered a greeting. He was waiting for Dry's order, which he knew would be a half pint. Dry never ordered more than a half, and seldom ordered more than once. What with that, and his strange mode of life, Amos disapproved of him almost completely.

'Mind if I join you?' Dry said when he had been given his ale.

'Not a bit,' Alison said, conscious that she was pleased to be asked by such a tall, striking man.

He folded himself on to the bench at her side. 'I'm surprised to find you here,' he remarked. 'I think of you as closed in behind the plate glass of the shop.'

'Oh, no, I escape sometimes.'

'Where to?'

'I beg your pardon?'

'Where do you fly to when you escape?'

'Oh . . . well . . . sometimes I come here for a quiet drink—'

'Which I'm interrupting. I'm sorry.'

'No, not a bit, I don't like to be *that* quiet! Sometimes I go for a walk—'

'Fishing?'

'Oh, so you've heard about that. Extraordinary. There's no bush here, so how can there be a bush telegraph?'

'And no grapes, so how can there be a grapevine? But a stroll to the Woolpack and an hour dangling a line in the river doesn't seem very adventurous. Don't you ever get the urge to live a little?'

'Frequently.'

'And what do you do then?'

'I come to terms with the facts of life and settle for a meal in a new restaurant.'

'Really? You like to try new places?'

'Well, yes.'

'Then will you allow me to take you to a special find of my own?'

'What?' Alison said faintly. It was totally unexpected.

'I'd like to take you out to a meal. Please say you'll come.'

'Well, I . . . I don't really know . . .'

'What don't you know?'

'Whether . . . whether I could fit it in.'

'Oh, greatly in demand, are you? You mean it's no good hoping you'll come out tonight?'

'I'm afraid not.'

'Tomorrow, then.'

'No, sorry.'

'Good gracious! Sunday, then?'

'But Dry . . . are you sure you . . .'

'What?'

She could scarcely ask him if he had the money to pay for a meal in a restaurant. Besides, would he ask her if he had no money? Even Dry, strange though he was, wouldn't inflict a scene over the bill upon her, nor expect her to wash dishes to pay for their meal.

'The Sugdens have asked me to do a conversion job in their attic,' he told her, perhaps totally at random and perhaps to reassure her on the money point. 'They need an extra bedroom.'

'Oh, yes, I've heard Annie and Joe discussing it. I didn't know you were an expert on that kind of thing?'

'You don't know what I'm expert in,' he said with a smile. 'Nor do I, if it comes to that. But I do know a good cook when I come across one – so will you come with me on Sunday evening and sample his cooking?'

'Very well, then,' she said, coming to a sudden and pleasurable decision, 'I will. Thank you, Dry. What time?'

'I'll let you know,' he told her. He finished his half and rose. 'I'd better get back to Emmerdale. I've got measurements to take for wood to do the conversion. I'll be in touch.'

The transport problem for Matt's date with Alison was solved by Christine Sharp, who lent Matt her smart little white sports car. When it drove up to the shop, Matt looked so incongruous in it that Alison couldn't help laughing aloud. Matt took it in good part.

'This is my Niki Lauda outfit,' he told her, indicating his tweed jacket and plain shirt.

'What, no crash helmet?' She got in beside him, intrigued to see where he would take her. She had a feeling that the choice of restaurant would owe something to Christine also, for Matt wasn't the kind of man who read the *Good Food Guide.*

It turned out to be a quiet, unassuming place in Hotten. The food was good and the wine more than adequate, but Alison's pleasure in the event was lessened by Matt's obvious uneasiness. He didn't know how to choose the dishes, and it took some diplomacy from her to guide him towards suitable items. The array of cutlery baffled him. The wine list meant nothing to him. Luckily the wine waiter took the matter in hand without being too uppish.

All in all, it was an evening that she couldn't entirely call a success. She had hoped to learn a lot more about Matt, who was always reticent about himself, but the setting wasn't quite right for him. He couldn't relax.

Matt himself was well aware that he didn't do well. As he drove her back to Emmerdale his mind was full of things he should have said. Too late now. The whole idea had been to get Alison to himself for an evening, three hours of uninterrupted talk that was impossible in Beckindale where they were so well known. He had the feeling he would have done better to take her to the pictures. They could at least have held hands there . . .

'Thank you for coming out with me,' he said as she got out by the shop door.

'Thank you for asking me. I enjoyed it.'

'Did you, Alison?' He was eager for her reassurance, even if he sensed that it wasn't entirely genuine.

'We must do it again some time,' she said.

No, he thought, as he drove on to the farm, not that again – that ordeal with funny French on the menu and waiters hovering over them. He was no good in a place like that. He'd never been in a restaurant – a proper restaurant, as opposed to a snack bar or a café – above twice in his life. Once was when he and Peggy were on their honeymoon, and they went to a posh place in Scarborough where she had ordered scampi to find out what it was . . .

Peggy . . . Oh, Peggy, why did you leave me? he thought as the sports car surged up the road to the only place in the world he could call home – a place where no woman waited for him.

CHAPTER THREE

Henry ushered Alison into the restaurant with a proprietorial air. 'I think you'll like this place,' he told her. 'I gather it's rather good though it doesn't look much of a spot.'

'How did you come to hear of it?' Alison inquired in a demure tone.

'Joe's girl-friend, Christine . . . I heard her mention it. Her father's Robert Sharp, the textile man, you know – she's been used to the good things of life.'

'I see.'

The head waiter hurried up to see them to their table. 'Good evening, sir,' he said. 'Good evening, madam. Nice to see you again.'

'Again?' Henry repeated, with a startled glance at Alison. But in the business of having chairs drawn out for them and menus thrust into their hands, he didn't have a chance to pursue the inquiry. He couldn't help noticing, though, that Alison was blushing a little under the gaze of the waiter.

Damned pretty she looked, he thought. Her soft hair was done up in loose curls, she was wearing a dress – a gown, should it be called? – of dark stuff that accentuated her grey eyes. He felt she had made a special effort on his behalf, and was pleased.

But 'again'? When had she been here before? And, more important, with whom?

One thing was comforting. He was sure she'd never been here with Matt Skilbeck. It was simply not his kind of place.

Reassured by this, Henry rather showed off while he was choosing the meal and ordering the wine. He was quite an expert on wine, after a lifetime spent in big business, and entertaining clients to expensive lunches. He murmured over the merits of the Rudesheimer Schlossberg as against the Wehlener Zeltinger Sonnenuhr, but finally settled on a bottle of the Château de Meursault '57. At one point he had a feeling that Alison was eyeing him with amusement, but when he glanced up he found she was sniffing the carnation in the slender vase on the table.

They ate their prawn cocktail while they chatted about the shop and minor matters. When the *boeuf bourgignon* was served, however, and the waiter had poured the wine, he felt they would be left in peace for a time.

He cleared his throat. 'You know, Alison, recently I've been trying to work out just where I'm going.'

'Going? You mean you're going away?'

He was pleased to hear a note of alarm in her tone. He shook his head. 'Nay, I was talking about the direction of my life, not my feet. I've settled here in Beckindale, you see, but when I first came it was with my daughter, to give her a new setting where she could forget an unhappy love affair.'

'And now she's gone.'

'Yes. Mind, I'm not saying I wouldn't have settled in the Dales anyhow. Always wanted to be a countryman, even when I was boxed up in an office in a high-rise block, making money over t'telephone. Outside, I could see clouds and the tops of trees, and I said to myself, "One day I'll walk under trees and look up at clouds, and there'll be no factory chimneys in the way . . ." '

'And you did it.'

'I usually do what I set my mind to,' he said, without false modesty. 'But you see, Alison . . . it's a sort of lonely life.'

She nodded. He knew he didn't have to describe to her what loneliness was. She too was alone, and alone in the most cruel way – her husband and child were dead because she had not been there to look after them, or so she thought. She had told him the story once. He had tried to urge upon her the view that she wasn't to blame, that her husband's treatment had brought her to an emotional confusion which had ended in her taking goods from a department store, and that in the time when she was serving the subsequent prison sentence her husband's negligence had caused the poisonous fumes in the heating system which had killed him and their child.

Over the past months, he had sensed that she was recovering from her guilt. In its way, life in Beckindale was busy and fulfilling. Henry had helped to keep it so, by buying a halfshare in the village shop when she couldn't afford to make the total purchase herself.

He went on now, 'I loved my wife. Always will, I suppose. When she died I never thought for a minute I'd ever want to marry again.'

'Henry, please . . .'

'Let me finish, Alison. I don't want to go over old history about what you said to me before, when I asked you. It's just that things have changed a bit – don't you think so? You said then you didn't feel like committing yourself. I'm hoping that . . .'

The words fell away. She was staring at him with eyes that glinted with tears. 'Please don't, Henry.'

Silenced, he looked down at his plate. The food suddenly looked unappetizing. He pushed it around with his fork.

'It's much better to leave things as they are,' she went on in a desperate, determined calm. 'I'm grateful to you for helping me, but there are some things I don't want between us, Henry.'

'But why not?'

'Because . . . because they get in the way of forgetting. When you speak of getting married again, you have to explain how you felt about your wife. I have to explain how I felt about Peter. I haven't got enough distance between me and what happened to be able to—'

'Dammit!' Henry exclaimed. 'Are you going to go on for the rest of your life blaming yourself?'

In the booth next to theirs, two other diners raised their heads at this explosion of sound. 'Heh,' muttered Joe Sugden, 'that's Henry!'

'So what?' Christine asked, smiling at him across the table.

'Nothing. Only . . . I wonder who he's with?'

'If he knew you were here, perhaps he'd wonder who you are with.'

'Nay,' Joe said. 'He'd know it had to be you.'

'That's nice, Joe. Thank you for saying that.'

Truth to tell, Joe had only meant that no one else he knew could have brought him to a restaurant like this. But he had enough sense to hold his tongue when the girl he was with thanked him for a compliment. He took the hand she held out, and told himself he was the luckiest man in the Dales this night, to have Christine Sharp sitting opposite him with that smile in her eyes.

'It's no use saying I shouldn't blame myself,' Alison said to Henry. 'And in a way that's not the point. The point is that I still miss Peter ... I'm sorry, Henry. When you spoke to me last time about how you felt, all I could think of was that you didn't really know me. You were angry when I explained, told me it didn't matter. And perhaps you were right – those months in gaol might never have been. But Peter is still there, in my mind, in my heart. And when I realized you still felt ... Well, I thought I ought to come out with you tonight, to explain.'

'Hmm ...' Henry said. In the face of a speech like that, it would be clumsy to insist on his own needs. After a moment he said, 'There's no one else?'

'No,' she said, surprised. 'No, Henry, there's no one else.'

'Thank heavens for small mercies,' Henry said, unfeelingly consigning Matt Skilbeck to insignificance. 'Let's have a bottle of champagne on that. Waiter!'

He raised his arm to flag the waiter. Joe, unable to ignore it, frowned at Christine. 'I feel like an eavesdropper,' he sighed.

'They're making a noise, it's not that we're listening!'

'But champagne,' Joe said. 'That means it's someone important.'

'You don't need champagne to make a girl feel important,' Christine told him, and leaned closer across the table.

It wasn't until Henry was ushering Alison out of the place that, in passing the next booth, he became aware that Joe and Christine were there. He was embarrassed, but hid it well.

'Hello, young Joe. Got good taste, haven't you?'

'Do you mean in my choice of restaurant or my choice of girl?' Joe parried, inspired by the surroundings and the good wine he had drunk.

'Both. 'Night, then.'

' 'Night, Henry.'

'That was Alison Gibbons from the village shop, wasn't it?' Christine asked as soon as the others were out of earshot.

'That's right. He's always been a bit keen on her. Thought last year he might actually pop the question.'

'And did he?'

'Dunno. If he did, she said no.' Joe pondered a moment. 'I

wonder if Matt knows Henry's still interested in Alison?'

'Does Henry know that Matt is interested?'

'That's a good question,' said Joe.

Another good question was whether either Henry or Matt knew that Dry was interested. They would both have been surprised if they had seen him arriving at the door of the shop on Sunday evening and being immediately opened to.

'Sssh,' said Alison, anxious to avoid the noise of the shop bell jangling in the Sunday silence.

'What's the matter?' Dry inquired. 'Is this a secret assignation?'

Alison was rather wondering if it was an assignation at all. Having been invited out, she had dressed for the occasion – a light wool dress with a silk scarf at the throat, and her best Jaeger coat. Dry, in contrast, was wearing his usual Norwegian sweater and corduroys.

'It won't be secret if we stand here on the doorstep much longer.'

'I hadn't exactly planned to spend our evening together on the doorstep. Are you ready?'

I am, thought, Alison. Are you? Aloud she said, 'Where are we going?'

He looked dubious. 'A lot depends on the shoes you're wearing.'

'Shoes?' she echoed, astounded.

'Let's have a look. Well, I've seen more suitable footwear, but t'will serve.'

'Are we going on a five-mile march?' she asked with apprehension.

'No, no, just to the crossroads to catch the bus.'

'The bus? There isn't a bus on Sunday.'

'Not through Beckindale, no. But if we walk to Billwell crossroads we can catch the Leeds bus.'

'We're never going to Leeds?'

'Certainly not. I never go into cities if I can avoid it.'

'So where, then? Are we going to . . . a roadhouse?'

'You might call it that.'

It proved to be a drivers' caff, set on a main road in the middle of a bleak stretch of moorland. From the outside it was the least prepossessing place Alison had ever seen. 'Are we . . .

are we going in there?' she asked in a tone of helpless disbelief.

'This is Chez Cloggett. You'll like it.'

'Cloggett?'

'That's what he calls himself and I believe him. Come on, a gastronomic treat awaits you.'

There was nothing to do but go with him. The extraordinary thing was that he turned out to be right: they were served the best mixed grill Alison had ever eaten in her life, together with two cups of hot strong tea which seemed to act on her like wine. As far as she could see, no money changed hands; Dry appeared to have done some service to Alfie Cloggett in the past which entitled him to a free meal whenever he wanted it. It even seemed that the place had opened specially for him, for no one else came in while they were there.

When time came for them to head for home, the enjoyment began to die out. 'Won't the last bus have gone?' she asked as he held her coat for her.

'I'm afraid so.'

'So what do we do?'

'Why do you think I asked if you were wearing sensible shoes?'

'You're not expecting me to walk the twelve miles to Beckindale?' she cried.

He laughed, with that sudden flash of white teeth in his dark beard. 'There is an alternative.'

'What?'

'Alfie has a couple of rooms above, that he lets out to lorry drivers.'

Her eyes went wide. But after a moment of staring at him in rather shocked silence, she realized that he wasn't serious.

'If I say no to that, what happens?' she asked.

'Well, I would have to be an honourable man and get you home to your own bed.'

'How, exactly?'

'Come and find out.'

They went out, calling goodnight to Alfie. They walked up the road in the cold winter air with the stars twinkling in the black sky overhead. Although she was a countrywoman by adoption now, there was a brooding stillness about this upland moor that frightened her. She took Dry's arm, and he drew her close.

'The gods of the wild places make themselves felt at times like this,' he murmured.

'It's . . . it's intimidating.'

'Only if you have reason to fear it. Moorland is where man has to treat nature with due regard – not like in the farming country where they can score it with ploughs, turn tame animals out on it . . . Here you have to respect the earth, and in return the earth gives you your freedom.'

'And is that what you want, Dry? Freedom?'

'Did you ever hear that great Scots poem? *Freedom is a noble thing, it maketh man to have liking* . . . Liking in that sense meaning a taste for living.'

'You're a strange man,' she murmured.

'Not a bit. Very normal, I assure you.' He drew her closer, and for one strange moment she thought he was going to kiss her, and had time for the totally feminine thought that it would be the first time she'd ever kissed a man with a beard.

And then the headlights of a heavy lorry burrowed into the darkness, silhouetting them. Dry didn't let her go – he was too unselfconscious to care about being outlined in the act of kissing a girl. But the moment had passed, and when the vehicle stopped at his signal, they clambered aboard in amicable silence.

That was the end of her evening out with Dry. The lorry-driver actually made a detour, under the blandishments of Dry, to drop them outside the shop. Although it was still early, Dry shook hands and said goodnight.

'I won't stay,' he teased, 'because you don't want me lingering on your doorstep. Until next time, Alison.'

'Goodnight, Dry – and thank you for a lovely evening.'

If she thought the events of the night had gone unnoticed, she under-estimated the interest that her neighbours took in her. Mrs Carley, who lived opposite, had seen her departure with her escort early on.

'Not going out with Mrs Gibbons this evening?' she inquired of Henry as she accepted her port and lemon in the bar of the Woolpack about seven o'clock, as usual.

Henry agreed that he was not. Being partner to Amos

Brearley in the Woolpack was much harder work than being partner to Alison in the shop – as co-landlord he had to be polite to everyone, even nosy parkers like Mrs Carley.

'Oh, no, of course not. It was last night you went out with her,' said that lady, enjoying herself. 'It's Mr Hogben tonight.'

'Hogben?' Henry jerked out. 'Dry Hogben?'

'That's him – him with the beard. Can't imagine where they'd be going, can you?'

'He took her out?'

'Over an hour ago,' she said, and sipped her drink.

Henry was astounded. Dry Hogben taking Alison out? What could she be thinking of, to accept an invitation from such a man. It spoiled the rest of Sunday evening for him.

Matt Skilbeck was spared the knowledge until later. About nine o'clock, restless and unable to settle to the film on Annie's television, he put on his coat and went out. He thought he might have a brisk walk, take a pint at the Woolpack, and on his way back see that the farm was locked up for the night.

This was how he saw Alison and Dry saying goodnight outside the shop. On the night air he heard her light voice, 'Goodnight, Dry, and thank you for a lovely evening.'

A lovely evening. Two nights ago he had taken her out. He was only too conscious that she couldn't have thanked him – with truth – for a lovely evening. It had been strained and awkward, he out of his depth and she anxious on his account.

It was useless. He was the wrong kind of man for such as Alison.

His shoulders hunched against the keen breeze, he turned and began to walk back to the farm.

Joe and Christine were out together. Sam had gone to bed. Annie was alone in the farm kitchen when he went in. 'Hello, you're back soon,' she said, looking round from the cooker where she was heating milk for her night-time drink.

He hung up his coat without replying.

'Were Joe and Christine in t'Woolpack?'

'I didn't go in.'

She heard the misery in his voice. Frowning to herself, she poured boiling milk on cocoa and sugar, and stirred. 'Like yours now?' she asked.

'No thanks, Ma.'

'I'll put milk in saucepan ready, shall I?'

'I'll not bother tonight.'

'Oh.' She took her mug to her chair and sat down. 'Everything all right, Matt?'

'Oh, aye.'

She sipped her cocoa, looking at him over the rim of the mug.

'Don't worry about me, Ma,' he said.

'Why not? I worry about everybody else.'

'Aye, and it's not right, that. It's not fair. You've your own life to lead.'

'And you've yours. I keep waiting to see you take hold of it again.'

He shrugged. 'I dunno,' he said. 'It's just that I don't feel I rightly belong anywhere any more.'

Annie gave him her cool, calm glance. 'You belong here, Matt. You know that.'

'Not the way Peggy did . . .'

'If that doesn't make you our family, what does?'

belong here as much as Joe or my father. Nothing's changed in that respect, though Peg's gone.'

'But I feel different, Ma. I feel . . . sort of lost. As if this isn't my family. And it isn't, if you think it through.'

'You've given me two lovely grandchildren,' she said gently. 'If that doesn't make you our family, what does?'

'But I can't even manage things so that you can have the twins here—'

'Most grandmothers don't have their grandchildren living with them, Matt. There's nowt unusual in that. It's *you* that makes the sacrifice, in staying with us while your children are elsewhere. I sometimes think you might leave us so as to set up some kind of a home for them.'

'Nay!' he said, shocked. 'It's the opposite – I want to bring them back here.'

'Then when Dry gets the loft converted, happen we can have them with us. That'll make things better.'

'Aye,' he agreed. But he sighed.

She took the plunge. 'If ever you thought of getting married again, Matt . . . eventually, I mean . . .'

He shrank away from the words. 'I can't seem to see that. I . . . I loved Peggy, Ma.'

'I know that, lad. And if one day you found another girl to love, she'd be welcome here. I want you to know that, Matt.'

'You'd be able to welcome a stranger here?'

'She wouldn't be a stranger if she were your wife.'

He hesitated. 'Sometimes, when I go for a walk, I go past Hawthorn. We've never touched it since Peg died. All that work I put in, and all for nothing.'

She understood that he wasn't complaining about wasted work. He was trying to voice a feeling that life had been unfair to Peggy, to take her from the home he had so lovingly furbished up for her. Poor, bright, busy Peggy. Annie felt tears prick behind her eyes.

'One day, happen you'll be able to go in there again, Matt. You might feel able to live there, even.'

He shook his fair head. 'I don't think so.'

With what for her was an unusual flight of fancy, Annie said, 'Ghosts shouldn't rule the living, Matt. If there are ghosts at Hawthorn, you ought to lay them to rest.'

He rose and made for the stairs. 'I think I'll go to bed now, Ma. I've had a busy day.'

'Goodnight then, Matt.'

'Goodnight, Ma.' He went slowly up the stairs. She heard his heavy footsteps and sat thinking about him while her nightcap grew cold. If he was attracted to Alison Gibbons, that could only be a good thing. Alison was a good lass, gentle, genuine, honest. She would make Matt a good wife.

If only . . . if only Matt could win her. And if he could not, that might well be worse for him than remaining faithful to the memory of Peggy.

He was competing with Henry to win Alison's affections. It was scarcely an equal contest, for Henry had worldly experience and money whereas Matt was reticent, shy, and not rich.

Perhaps he needed some help. Little though Annie thought of herself in the role of matchmaker, perhaps she ought to take a hand. Yes, why not? She and Matt against Henry Wilks – that ought to even up the odds a little!

But help or no help, the final question was Alison. How did she feel about Matt? About Henry? There was some mystery in her past that Annie didn't understand and would never dream of inquiring into. But whatever it was, it had scarred Alison.

Why else was she here, living alone in a little village in the Dales – a pretty, intelligent woman like that? She could have held her own in a big city, made a career for herself.

No, something had happened to Alison, something bad. Yet in a way that made her all the more right for Matt. Matt had suffered. Something within him ought to call to Alison.

But even so, Annie told herself with level-headed foresight, even the best matched pair will never come together unless the opportunity is there. It was time to give Matt some opportunity to court Alison Gibbons. The first chance she got, Annie was going to get Matt and Alison together.

Perhaps it was as well that Annie had decided to throw herself into the fight, for as he lay in his bed that night staring up at the ceiling, Matt was admitting defeat. It was wild talk, saying to Annie that he might bring a new wife to Emmerdale. Alison would be giving up too much – it was unreasonable to suggest it. Now if Henry were to ask her, he could offer her so much . . .

Facing it honestly, you had to admit: Alison would be a fool to refuse Henry. And it was clear Henry was going to propose. The minute he did, it would be settled, Alison would say yes, and Matt's dream would be over.

Better to accept it now. It would save heartache later. He would step back from the contest while he still had nothing to lose, before he began building too many dream castles.

Yes, that was sense.

But it was no consolation.

CHAPTER FOUR

A strange event took place in the Emmerdale household. Not so strange, really – for the Bible has something to say about the way of a man with a maid, after all . . . But when Joe went one Saturday afternoon to view the model farm owned by Christine's father, Annie wasn't thinking about the *Book of Proverbs.*

He rang about nine o'clock in the evening to say that Christine's car had broken down and that therefore they'd be unable to get back. When Annie, with compressed lips, resumed her seat after taking this message, neither Old Sam nor Matt dared remark that there must be other transport on such a fine estate – the farm manager's, for instance, who lived in a cottage the far side of the place. And there was always the telephone, by means of which it was possible to summon a hire car.

Somehow it made for a feeling of tension in the Emmerdale kitchen. Sam got up, stretching and holding his arms above his head. 'Well, what d'you say, Matt? Fancy a pint at the pub?'

Matt met his eye. 'Why not?' he agreed.

It was a good move. That happened to be the night that Henry decided to make a public announcement in the bar that he and Amos were in partnership and offered drinks on the house to all their customers. Coming in a moment later and unaware of what had happened, Matt espied Alison.

Somehow heartened or liberated by Joe's act, Matt went over to her. 'Hello, Alison! How you been?'

'I'm fine,' she said, smiling in delight. It had been so long since Matt had said more than a polite good-day . . . not since that awkward evening at the restaurant, in fact.

'What are you having?' he asked.

'Oh . . . I think a shandy.'

'Nay, I'm buying. Have summat better than that!'

'No, Matt—'

'Dry Martini, that's what you like. I remember . . . I'm having a double rum.' To celebrate, he might have added – to celebrate the fact that I've met you again.

He made his way to the bar and put his order. Amos nearly fainted. 'Rum?' he gasped.

'A double, please, Amos,' said the innocent Matt, putting his hand in his pocket.

'Nay, lad,' Henry put in. 'On the house tonight.'

'On the house?'

'Aye, to celebrate our partnership, Amos and me.'

Matt suddenly felt that everything was coming up roses. To accept Sam's invitation to go down to the Woolpack, to find Alison there, to be greeted by her with so much warmth, and then to get the drinks free—! With a smile on his broad face, he struggled back to Alison. 'Cheers!' he said with fervour.

When he and Sam got home Annie was still up. Matt was so pleased with himself that she couldn't fail to notice it. 'Had a good time?' she asked.

He explained about the free drinks. 'Amos nearly died,' he chuckled. 'Alison tried to warn me, but I didn't stop to listen. You should have seen his face when I asked for a double rum and a Martini.'

'Saw Alison, did you? How is she?'

'Fine, I think. But it's hard to have a conversation in a saloon bar.'

Annie took the necessary step. 'You should invite her here,' she said.

'Here?'

'Why not?'

He knew what it meant. In a way Annie was giving him permission to court Alison. He stretched out his legs towards the fire and thought about it.

'May do,' he said.

Joe and Christine turned up halfway through next morning. Annie greeted them with complete warmth and openness. In view of her attitude, no one dared to make any allusions to the previous night.

While they were doing the evening milking, Matt said, 'What's Sharp's farm like then?'

'Tremendous! Chris doesn't like it, but I wish we could get half the results here . . .'

'What was wrong with her car then?'

'The plugs were damp. I dried 'em out this morning.'

'Oh aye?'

'Aye.'

Matt went to examine the dials at the far end of the parlour. 'Had a nice time then?'

'We had a great time.'

'That's all I were asking,' Matt protested.

'And that's all I'm telling,' replied Joe.

Matt thought it over that evening as he drove to Middleton's to visit Auntie Beattie and Uncle Ben and the twins. These days, everything was so easy. Joe could spend a night with a girl and no one said a thing. Why then should he be so shy about being attracted to Alison? It wasn't a crime, hang it, to like a woman, to want to be with her.

But not in a posh restaurant. Oh no. Once bitten, twice shy. Next time he asked Alison for a meal, it would be somewhere that he could be at ease.

However, it's one thing to say brave things like that to yourself, and quite another to carry them into practice. The days went by, and he couldn't think of any place to invite Alison to. He thought of the cinema, but when he investigated the programmes he decided that he would rather die than see any of them. As to taking a respectable woman – that was impossible! He began looking at the gourmet column in the local paper to see what restaurants were recommended, but they said things like: 'The wine list is adequate, the Hungarian Riesling is not remarkable but will pass.' What the devil was Hungarian Riesling? Did you eat it or drink it?

One afternoon he went into the shop on some pretext. Mrs Prescott was there, Mrs Prescott with whom Dry Hogben was rumoured to be carrying on an affair – though how it could be true Matt didn't know for Dry was mostly hard at work in the attic at Emmerdale. Mrs Prescott was a rather aggressively handsome woman who had moved out of Bradford to enjoy the country air. Matt, who saw more than he let on, rather thought she had moved out to Beckindale in hopes of getting her husband away from the cocktail-party set.

Diana Prescott was laying in supplies for a house-warming. 'We've just got straight enough to invite some friends in,' she explained. 'Dry's done the re-wiring, and my husband's actually finished painting the living-room, so I thought I'd take the plunge. I've made a simply enormous list – I hope you'll have at least some of these things.'

'These things' turned out to be foods that Matt had never heard of. Lumpenfisch, *bisque d'homard*, roquefort, asparagus tips – well, yes, he'd heard of asparagus tips. But most of the items were rich and strange.

When she had gone, her basket brimming with goodies, Matt said to Alison, 'That's fancy stuff, isn't it?'

'Yes, but very enjoyable.' She smacked her lips.

'You like that kind of thing?'

'Of course. Nice work if you can get it.'

'You got another lot?'

'Another lot of what?'

'Of those things. The same again, I mean.'

'Same again. You mean a duplicate order? Well ... Yes, I reckon I have. Why?'

'I'd like to have all that. Put it in a carton for me, will you, Alison? I'll take it home to Annie.' He took a deep breath. 'And you come to tea tonight.'

'What?' It was an exclamation bordering on dismay.

'Come to tea. We'll have all them things you like.'

'Tonight?' she almost squeaked.

'Yes, why not?'

'But . . . but . . . won't Annie need some warning?'

'Nay,' he said, with sublime confidence in his mother-in-law's ability to surmount any crisis. 'She told me to invite you any time.'

'But, Matt—'

'Don't you want to come?' he interrupted.

'Of course I do. But—'

'That's settled then. I'll fetch you, shall I? Six o'clock.'

'Yes,' she said faintly, 'six o'clock.'

When Annie Sugden saw the box of groceries, she almost failed to live up to Matt's expectations. 'You've bought all this?' she asked, shaken.

'Aye. Alison says she likes that kind of thing. I knew you wouldn't mind.'

'No, I don't mind,' Annie said. 'What time's she coming?'

'Six o'clock.'

'I see.' She made rapid calculations. Goodbye to the rabbit

pie she was going to put on the table. It would hardly go with Lumpenfisch roe and *bisque d'homard.* Asparagus tips – a tiny tin enough for two! What was she supposed to do with that when she was catering for six? Seven, perhaps, if Henry came by as he so often did at mealtimes.

She laboured manfully. She eked out the lobster soup with poached whiting, she made a winter salad with diced carrots and peas and the asparagus tips, she put the black fish roe out on little biscuits because, in her opinion, it looked like some kind of caviare and she had read that caviare was eaten on biscuits or snippets of toast. For the main course she devised a veal stew that would be easy on the digestion after these rich preliminaries. The sweet was frozen raspberries and water ice; what her father and her son Joe would say to such things she couldn't imagine.

To make certain that at least her father wouldn't spoil everything, she warned him beforehand. 'Matt's paid for all this with his own money,' she told him, 'so no daft remarks, Dad.'

'Paid for it, has he?' Sam said, glaring at the spread on the table. 'More fool he! What kind of a tea is that? Where's the fruit cake?'

'You don't have fruit cake after a meal like this, Dad.'

'Ee,' groaned Sam, 'I know what I'll have after a meal like this. I'll have the—'

'Dad!' she exclaimed, holding up a finger.

He was silent. She only wished she could have had the chance to forewarn Joe, but he was out somewhere with Christine. When he turned up, Alison and Matt were with him. Somehow the whole gathering seemed alight with unexpressed happiness. While Annie put the finishing touches, Christine sat down to the old piano in the parlour; it was strange, nostalgic, heartwarming to hear the voices raised in song again – like old times, like the days before Peggy died.

But she mustn't think about Peggy. This was the evening when Matt had brought Alison to be shown to the family as a prospective member. Alison might not be aware of that, but Annie was, and so was Sam. She would hear her father now, singing 'My love's an Arbutus' – that had been her mother's favourite song.

Yes, dad knew it was a family occasion, she thought. Let's hope it all goes well.

They sat down to the meal. She was handing round the soup tureen when Dry Hogben walked in. In the excitement, she had quite forgotten that he was working quietly up there in the attic. 'Good gracious!' she cried, staring up. 'Dry! And we've all just started our teas!'

'Why don't you join us?' Joe invited, waving a hand at the table. 'Plenty here!'

Dry surveyed them all quizzically. It struck Annie that his eye rested a little longer on Alison than the others. 'I'd love to,' he said. 'May I wash up first?'

'Oh . . . please . . . you'll find a clean towel on the bath . . . we'll wait for you.'

'Don't be long,' called Joe.

He was back by the time the soup had been served. Annie gave him the tureen and he helped himself. 'Well,' he commented, 'this looks like a celebration.'

'It's nowt special,' Matt murmured.

'It looks special to me. Nobody has any special news?' Once more he looked at Alison, but Alison was busy sampling the *bisque d'homard et de merlan.*

'Well, if nobody else has, I have,' Joe exclaimed.

'Joe!' cried his mother, divided between eagerness and dismay at what she guessed was coming.

'Where is it?' Joe said to Christine.

'In the freezer.'

'The freezer? It'll explode!' He rushed away, while everyone except Annie sat looking bewildered. In a moment he was back with a bottle of champagne held aloft.

'What's that for?' his grandfather demanded in a quelling tone.

'What d'you think? We're engaged!'

Christine blushed and laughed, the table exploded in congratulations, Dry for some reason looked relieved. After a moment Annie spared a glance for Matt. He was wryly watching the handshaking that was going on.

'I'll get the glasses,' he said, and got up.

As he got them out of the sideboard in the parlour he couldn't help a little laugh of self-derision. 'Always the bridesmaid, never the bride, that's me,' he thought. Wasn't it just typical, that the special tea he'd planned for Alison should turn out to be someone else's engagement party? With a short sigh, he took the stems of the glasses between his fingers and went with them to the table. Joe was struggling with the cork. It flew out with a satisfactory pop and champagne went brimming over the neck of the bottle.

But for Matt the fizz had gone out of the occasion.

All the same, he had made a step forward. It might have proved a stumbling progression, but he had actually invited Alison to Emmerdale as his own special guest. And now marriage was in the air. Christine and Joe talked about it all the time.

Henry Wilks couldn't help but notice that there had been a change in the relationship between Matt and Alison. How it had come about he wasn't quite sure, but somehow now they seemed to have things in common – they would refer back to conversations they had, or fail to finish sentences as if each knew what the other had been going to say.

He found it worrying, upsetting. After Alison told him over their restaurant meal that she didn't want to be pressed on the subject of marriage, he had respected her wishes. He had widened the gap between them a little. But that didn't mean he wanted another man walking into the gap he had left.

Going past the shop one evening, he saw the light still on. He frowned, stopped, and knocked. Alison opened to him. 'Saw the light,' he remarked. 'Wondered what you were up to.'

'Stocktaking,' she explained. She had a smut of dust on her nose and a clipboard in her hand. 'It's quite a job,' she went on. 'There are thousands of items. We'll have to cut down the range of goods, Henry.'

'You should have asked,' he said, taking off his coat. 'I'll give you a hand.'

'As a matter of fact I—'

'Shall I call and you mark, or what?'

'There's no need, Henry. I can manage.'

'Nonsense. It's as much my responsibility as it is yours. I ought to help you more here but somehow . . . I dunno . . .' He looked over her shoulder at the clipboard. 'Cereals, is it? Right . . .'

'I've done those,' she said, in a tone that ought to have told him he wasn't really wanted.

'Oh, I see. Tinned goods. Right. Here . . .' He went to the shelves behind the freezer and began to count. 'Pilchards, seven-and-a-half ounce size, four, eight, sixteen tins. Pilchards, fifteen ounces, two, times four on this shelf, times two shelves, sixteen tins again, that's the pilchards. Seven-and-a-half ounces – what a daft weight for a tin of summat! Better when we get metrication after all! Sardines, one carton, that's two dozen. Herrings in tomato, large size only, one carton – no, wait, there's sardines stacked on top.'

'Please, Henry!' cried Alison, her pencil wavering over the stocktaking list. 'I can't find them here—'

'Going too fast, am I?'

'There's no hurry. I think I'll do better on my own, really.'

'But two heads are better than one . . .'

'I quite agree – but it depends on which heads,' she replied, laughing a little.

But Henry didn't laugh. 'You mean you could think of someone you'd rather have helping you?'

'Oh, no, I—'

'You just said – "it depends on which heads" – that means you don't like me being here helping.'

'I didn't say that, Henry—'

'That's what it sounded like to me!'

'I only meant that I—'

'You've got someone else coming?'

'No – yes – I don't really need—'

'Is Matt Sugden coming?'

She was silent.

'Did you ask Matt to help you?'

'I don't know. He offered.'

'And that's why you were anxious to get rid of me?'

'Nothing of the kind!' she cried, startled. 'It's just that—'

'You told Matt you were going to do the stocktaking. You didn't tell me.'

'It just happened. He was in the shop when I was preparing—'

'Oh, yes, he was in the shop. He's in the shop a lot these days.'

'It's not a crime, Henry,' she said, stiffening.

Henry picked up his coat and began to put it on again. He tried to get hold of himself. He knew he had blundered in where he wasn't expected and had reacted badly. After a moment he said, 'That night in the restaurant, when we had dinner . . .'

'Yes?'

'You said there was no one else.'

'That was true, then. But things change.'

'Pretty quickly,' he said, too angry to take as much care as the situation demanded. 'You were out with Matt the next night.'

'No, Henry, I was out with Dry Hogben, the next night,' she corrected him, her manner chill.

'Oh, him . . .' He made a dismissive gesture. Dry didn't bother him half as much as Matt, who had so many claims on a woman's affections. 'Do you deny that you've been going out with Matt?'

'Deny it? Of course I don't deny it,' she rejoined.

'I just expected you to be honest with me, that's all.'

'I can only be as honest as the moment,' she said. 'When you asked me that time if there was anyone else, I told you honestly that there wasn't. Since then, things have altered – I can't say how much, but they *have* altered. What did you want me to do – give you a daily report?'

'When I asked you that question I was thinking about marriage, Alison. You knew that.'

'Yes.'

'I took it to mean there was no one you were thinking of marrying.'

'And I answered you in that sense.'

'Is that still how things are?'

It dawned on Alison that they were on the verge of a big row. She curbed her irritation to say, defensively, 'It's nothing to do with you, Henry.'

'You've got your eye on Matt, the way I see it.'

She laid her clipboard on the counter then looked up at him. He saw a glint in her grey-blue eyes that he had never expected to see – at least, not directed against him.

'I think you'd better go, Henry,' she said.

'Not before I've had some kind of an explanation.' He couldn't listen to his better sense, which was telling him to break off the encounter. 'After all, you've known for a long time that—'

'I owe you nothing – nothing at all. And you have no right to try and take over control of my private life. Are you saying I have no right to be friends with a man unless I have your permission? Are you going to dictate to me whom I should meet? Am I to tell you about anyone new that I meet, before I engage in a friendly chat with him?'

'Oh, now, Alison—'

'You are a nice man, Henry,' she went on, disregarding his faint protest. 'I like you. But please don't try to run my life for me.'

'I wasn't,' he said, although he knew it was untrue. 'I was only—'

'You were telling me that I had more or less promised to give you first refusal.'

'Oh, I didn't mean anything of the sort—'

'What else did you mean? You reminded me that I had said there was no one else. That was some weeks ago. You're angry because now there *may* be someone. You seem to imply that you should have been told.'

'I didn't need to be told,' he groaned. 'I could see it happening. You and Matt—'

'I've been spending a lot of time talking to Dry, too. He's a very interesting man. Do I take it you disapprove of that?'

'Dry's different,' Henry blurted. 'I can't see Dry ever proposing marriage. But Matt—'

'But Matt could very well ask me to be his wife, and you want to prevent that – is that it? What right have you got to want to prevent something that Matt may do?'

'I don't mind his asking you! What I'd mind is if you said yes!'

'But you'd have no right to mind. I've never promised you that I'd either remain a widow or accept your offer, Henry. Have I?'

'No-o-o,' he admitted. 'No, I've never imagined that you were tied to any such arrangement. It's just that . . .'

'What?'

'I do feel I have some claim.'

'We'd better end this conversation,' she said in a tone of ice.

'Nay, Alison—!'

There was a tap on the outer door. 'Alison!' Matt called from outside.

She went at once to let him in. 'By gow, there's a wind coming up,' Matt said as he entered, rubbing his hands. 'Oh, hello, Henry. You going to help too?'

'I was,' Henry replied, turning away, 'but I daresay you can manage without me.' He walked out without another word.

'What's up wi' him?' Matt asked, astounded.

'Oh, he's got things on his mind. Business things,' she added, anxious not to provoke any inquiry.

'Poor old Henry. Trouble with him is, he's got his finger in too many pies,' Matt remarked, taking off his jacket. 'Likes to have control of things, does Henry.'

'Henry does like to be in control,' she agreed. 'How are the twins?'

'Fine, fine.' He hesitated. 'You must come and get to know them, Alison. I've been thinking . . .'

'What?'

'They'd like you.'

She smiled. 'I hope so.'

'Would you like to come and spend an afternoon with them?'

'Could I?' she asked, suddenly eager.

'Why not? I generally go over to Middleton's Farm two or three times in the week – just for an hour or so, when I can manage it. But I like to take them out for an afternoon now and again, to sort of have 'em to myself, away from Auntie Beattie. How would you like to come out and make it a foursome?'

'I'd love it!'

'Your next half-day then?'

'Next Wednesday? Yes, that would be fine. I was going to spend it dressmaking, but that can wait!'

'Great,' he said, grinning with delight. He turned to the shelves. 'What do we do, like? Do I tell you what's here and you mark in the numbers?

'That's it. But don't go too fast.'

'Nay, no danger of that. Let's see then . . . tinned goods.

Pilchards in little tins – one, two, three, four – that's sixteen tins. The label says seven and a half ounces. Got that?'

'Yes, thanks. Next along and on the shelf below – same number of large size tins?'

'Aye, that makes sixteen again, doesn't it? Fifteen ounces, they are. What's next? Sardines in a cardboard box. You haven't opened that yet. Doesn't anyone buy sardines?'

'Quite the opposite. I've had to bring in a new box because I sold out. Haven't had time to open it yet.'

'Shall I open it for you?' He prised up the flaps of the carton. 'Not keen on them myself,' he said. 'Olive oil – it always seems too rich for me. You can get 'em in tomato too, can't you?'

'Yes, that's right, but Dry has been buying the other kind. He seems to eat out of tins, mainly.'

'Aye . . .' Matt began to take the sardines out of the carton and stack them neatly on the shelf. 'A rum chap is Dry. D'you know he's sleeping up in our attic at Emmerdale now?'

'Is he?' she said, surprised.

'Oh, I thought he'd have told you. His tent got blown away. He's using the attic but beds down in a sleeping-bag.'

'He's a character,' she laughed.

Matt nodded. 'Seen a bit of the world, by the way he talks.'

'So I gather. He told me the other day that he'd seen sardines being caught.'

'Fancy that . . . I wonder what they look like when they're alive?' He examined the tins. 'Produce of Portugal. Dry's been to Portugal, then.'

'A lot of other places too, he tells me.'

'Oh?' Matt hesitated. 'He comes in the shop a lot, does he?'

'Of course. He buys things to eat, and occasional extras like batteries for his torch.' All at once, she decided to answer the questions that Matt would never ask. 'He'll be gone one day,' she said. 'He's the restless type.'

'You reckon?'

'When he's finished the loft conversion. Or even before that, if it bores him.'

'Nay, he'll do t'job,' Matt objected. 'He's promised he will, and he's the kind of chap that keeps his promises.'

'I wonder?' she mused. 'I can't help feeling he's turned his back on something or someone – and that implies promises broken, even if they're unspoken ones.'

Matt stood back to survey his row of sardine tins. 'You know a lot about Dry?' he queried.

'Enough to like him a lot and worry a little. I can't help feeling he's throwing away his life.'

'Well, it's his to throw away, I suppose.'

'That's right. And that's why I think he'll move on by and by – it's part of his problem, this rootlessness.'

'It wouldn't bother you if he moved on?'

'No,' she said with complete calm. 'I'd miss him, I suppose. Unusual conversation is always stimulating. But other people have come and gone – look at Jack.'

'Oh aye, Jack! Hard to remember that he's Annie's son!'

'What's he doing?'

'Last I heard, he was helping to write a film script in Rome. Dunno whether he was getting on with it – Annie read out a description of the office where they'd set him up. It sounded great. Joe reckoned it must be as big as the Middletons' barn!'

'Joe never wishes he'd done what Jack did – left Emmerdale for the big world outside?'

'Nay, Joe's like me. He can't imagine himself working indoors. I never can understand how a feller like Jack can sit down at a typewriter and spend all day there. Must be like being in prison, I reckon.'

To his surprise, Alison's head jerked up. Then after a moment she said slowly. 'Not quite. Nothing's as bad as being in prison.'

He looked at her with concern. 'You all right? You look a bit done in, all of a sudden.'

'I'm quite all right. Shall we start on the next shelf?'

'Sure you're not a bit overtired?'

'No, I'm fine,' she insisted.

But as he began to count out the next items, on the stock-list under her pencil she could see, as if on a diagram, the outline of the open prison where she had spent six months less remission for exemplary conduct.

CHAPTER FIVE

To seek solace after his row with Alison, Henry found himself heading for Emmerdale. He couldn't face his 'home', the Woolpack, with its crowd of affable drinkers. Yet again he felt keenly the lack of a place of his own, a place where he indubitably belonged and where someone – a special someone – waited for him.

Why had Alison rebuffed him like that? He was sure she had led him to expect . . .

He was angry with her. But even more, he was angry with himself. How could he have lost his touch so suddenly – the touch which had always helped him to handle people all through his business life? The reason was that this time he had been personally involved; it wasn't a case here of profit or loss on a balance sheet, it had been his whole future at stake.

Had he lost her? Had he antagonized her once for all? Please God, he prayed, don't let her turn away from me. Then he found himself smiling a little in the darkness. Who was he to address pleas to the Almighty! A regular churchgoer, true, and a chorister whose hearty baritone would be missed if he left the choir – but there was no reason to suppose God took any special interest in his courtship of Alison Gibbons. Yet he had felt – or fooled himself that he felt – a sense of its being 'meant' for Alison and himself to marry.

He was alone. She was alone. He knew about her past – she herself had asked the vicar to tell him. He thought they were drawn to each other. Yes, they had been linked by some bond, however unstated. Until Matt came along.

Well, of course, Matt had always been there. It was only now, for some strange reason, that he had become important, had grown to be a threat.

A threat! How could anyone speak of Matt in that way? Matt was as good as home-made bread, as steady as Beckindale church, as unassuming as a tree that fitted into the landscape. Matt meant Henry no harm. Matt was no threat.

Yet for the first time in his life Henry Wilks found himself hard put to it not to dislike a man who had done him no intentional harm.

At Emmerdale he found Annie sitting in the kitchen listening to the radio. Overhead were sounds of activity. Henry, tilting his head, looked a question at her.

'Grandad and Dry,' she explained, on something of a sigh. 'Dry's taken some slates off the roof—'

'What on earth for?'

'He says he needs height to manoeuvre some of the beams he's taken up there. *I* don't know,' she said. 'I suppose it's necessary.'

'Still think he knows what he's doing?'

'I've confidence in Dry,' she said. 'But Grandad is convinced his bed is going to get soaked if it rains. His bedroom's directly underneath the hole that Dry's making in t'roof.'

Old Sam came surging in. 'I'm not having this!' he cried. 'He says the hole's for a window, Annie! I'm not having a hole that big—'

'But there's got to be a window, Sam,' Henry said, suddenly able to picture what Dry was doing in the attic.

'Why does he have to put it right over my bed?'

'But your bed is on the floor below—'

'If rain comes in, it'll find its way to the floor below. Water always finds its own level. Heh, Annie, you go up and talk to him. He'll heed what you tell him!'

She shook her head. 'I'm not interfering, Grandad. Come on now, sit thee down. I'll make a cup of tea.'

'Huh!' her father said, sinking into his armchair with a grunt of annoyance.

'Or would you like something stronger?'

'Stronger?' Henry echoed, astounded. It was the first time since he knew her that he had ever heard Annie offer strong drink.

'There's something left over from Christmas,' she explained, going into the parlour and returning with a whisky bottle about half full.

'Eeh, Annie!' Sam said, cheering up. He glanced at Henry. 'You gave us that. Having some, are you?'

'I wouldn't say no. Things have sort of got on top of me today.'

'Me too,' groaned the old man. He watched with an eagle eye as his daughter poured the drinks, hoping to get a measure that would equal his distresses.

'You having water with this?' she asked.

'Nay, it'll do my chest good to take it neat.'

'You, Henry?'

'I'll drink it straight, Annie.' He couldn't plead that he needed it for his chest, but he certainly felt it would do him more good as a stiff tot.

It then occurred to him as Annie put water in her own glass that it was very unusual indeed to see Annie drink.

'You been having a bad day?' he asked.

'Oh . . . well . . . it's all this planning of the marriage . . .'

'How'll you feel once Joe's a married man?'

She sipped, and thought about the question. 'I like Christine,' she said. 'She's a nice girl, and a real worker, but . . . I can't say I fancy her father in the family.'

'Oh aye,' Henry said, 'you've met him, you said?'

'Came here,' Sam put in, 'trying to tell Annie what to do, ordering her to fetch Christine into the house so he could lecture her—'

'Now, Dad, you know that was only because he was upset. But all the same, from what Christine says I gather he's a very difficult man. He more or less turned her out of the home . . . Well, what he'll say when he knows she's engaged to Joe, I dread to think.'

'You mean they haven't told him yet?'

She shook her head. 'They've been trying to phone him. He won't speak to Joe – either he's in a meeting or he's just gone out.'

'Well, the lad should leave a message asking him to ring back.'

'Do you think he hasn't? But Mr Sharp just ignores him.'

Henry blew out his breath and looked perturbed at the news. There was a silence.

'Why aren't you drinking at t'Woolpack?' Sam suddenly inquired.

'Felt like a change.'

'Oh? You missed your lady-friend, then.'

'What?' Henry asked, on a rising note of annoyance.

'Alison – she and Matt are going there after they've done this stocktaking thing. That's what Matt said, isn't it, Annie?'

His daughter gave him a little shake of the head. Sam, who either didn't see it or didn't choose to, went on, 'Thought you'd have been in on the stocktaking do, Henry. It's half your shop, after all.'

'I looked in,' Henry said, recovering himself. 'She didn't need me.'

Sam was going to probe further, but Annie turned the topic to the selling of sheep, planned for next market day. At length Henry drank up and moved to go. 'Tell Joe I'll see him about the sheep in t'morning.'

As the door closed on him Sam savoured the last of his own drink. 'Didn't look too happy to me,' he remarked.

Annie privately agreed. When her grandfather had spoken of Matt and Alison, Henry had looked down at his drink with a face suddenly grey. What a coil, she thought – if Matt takes Alison's fancy and makes a match of it, at poor Henry's expense ...

In the Woolpack, Alison and Matt went to slake their thirst after an hour's dusty work with the contents of the old shop's store room. To Matt's disappointment, Alison insisted on being content with a half of shandy. He brought it to her and sat opposite her at a table in a corner, his own pint of brown ale before him.

'Amos asked me if I was buying a dry Martini for you,' he told her. 'He was mad when I said you only wanted a shandy. He'll never forgive me for that night when the drinks were on the house.'

Alison laughed. 'Never mind, he'll do well out of drinks when the cricket season starts. Mrs Prescott's got her husband to join the cricket team, I hear – now *she's* a Martini drinker, I'm sure.'

'Aye, what do you think?' Matt said. 'Dry tells me he's talked her into joining the choir.'

'The church choir?'

'That's it. Told her she ought to take part in the community.'

'Be more to the point if he would join the choir,' Alison murmured. 'It might make him settle down.'

'Thought he might settle for a while anyway,' Matt said, watching her. 'Once he began getting friendly with Mrs Prescott.'

To his surprise, Alison giggled. 'A lot of my customers hint to me about a torrid affair between Dry and Mrs Prescott,' she said, 'but you can't really believe it when he's persuaded her into joining the church choir. Hardly seems to fit, does it?'

'No-o,' Matt agreed, smiling broadly. He felt he had quite a lot to smile about. No woman who felt attracted to a man could speak so calmly about a supposed love affair between Dry and Diana Prescott.

Following a train of thought of his own, he said after a few seconds' silence, 'Did you get married in church?'

She was taken aback. After a hesitation she said, 'Yes.'

'Do you believe in that sort of thing?'

'You mean in God?'

'More than that,' Matt said. 'I mean . . . Do you think people ought to get married in church?'

'Well, perhaps it's not necessary. But it's nice.' She looked for a phrase. 'I've always . . . kept in touch with the church.'

'Oh aye, Mr Ruskin is a good friend of yours, isn't he?'

'He told you that?' she riposted, her voice suddenly sharp.

Matt was surprised at the violence of her reaction. 'No, I don't think . . . I don't believe I've ever spoken to Mr Ruskin about you, Alison. It's just that I . . . I seem to remember that he recommended you for the job with Amos when you first came to Beckindale.' He laboured on, trying to undo the harm he had done, although in what way he didn't quite understand. 'I remember we had quite a joke about it, when you were first mentioned – the idea of Amos having a barmaid, you know . . . and you did live with Mr and Mrs Ruskin for a bit, didn't you?'

She was silent for a moment. She knew she had made a fool of herself by speaking so sharply.

'I was a parishioner of his before he came here,' she said.

'Did he marry you?'

'No.'

'He married me and Peg. Sugdens and almost everybody in Beckindale have been married in that church. In fact, Annie was telling me there's five generations of Sugdens buried in the churchyard. That's something, isn't it?' He was talking partly to allay the strange tension that had come over Alison since he first mentioned Mr Ruskin, and partly because now he thought of it, it was worth relating. 'I'm glad now I got twins baptized. It's part of belonging, isn't it? Baptized and wed and buried, all in the same parish. It's what makes things worth working for, living as part of a place like Beckindale, open to everyone to know your family and your worth. See what I mean, Alison?'

She made no reply. She looked quite pale.

'Are you all right?' he said, suddenly concerned.

'I'm rather tired. Would you mind if I went home?'

'No, of course not. Come on, I'll take you.' He put a hand under her elbow and guided her to the door of the saloon bar.

Neither he nor Alison saw Henry, who had come in through the living quarters and was watching as Matt gently helped Alison to reach the fresh air outside.

Once there, he expected to escort her to her door. But she seemed to hesitate. Despite herself, she was unwilling to go back to the cosy loneliness of the shop. Besides, it wasn't necessary now – the danger was past.

'Let's go for a walk,' she said. 'I could do with the fresh air.'

'Yes, that's a good idea. It was silly, really, to go into the muggy atmosphere of t'Woolpack after being cooped up in t'shop.'

'Cooped up!' she laughed, her composure restored. 'An hour or so indoors and you're straining at the leash.'

'Aye, it always seems cramped to me, working indoors.' They strolled out of the village towards Gimbel's Farm, where the moonlight glinted on the white fleece of the quiet sheep. On the bridge over the river, they paused to look at the sparkling dark water.

'Funny how things change,' Matt said, watching the current take a spray of leaves away. 'I used to come here with Peg . . .'

'You think of her a lot, don't you, Matt?'

'Every day,' he said simply. 'When she died, I thought I wouldn't live through another month, let alone a year . . .'

She nodded. In the dimness her face was unreadable. 'It was the same for me, with Peter.'

A long pause ensued. The only sound was the chuckle of the

water and a faint rustle from the trees. 'You don't think it's . . . disloyal, Alison?'

'What?'

'To . . . well . . . to get over missing someone?'

'You could never be disloyal, Matt,' she said in a low voice. 'I'm sure of that.'

'I don't think you could be either.' As she seemed to shake her head he went on quickly, 'Nay, you're too honest, Alison.'

Honest? The word gave her a stab of pain. She looked away. She gathered strength to say, 'You don't know me at all, Matt.'

But before she could utter the words, he said, 'I'm right, aren't I? You feel the way I do.'

'About what?' she parried, deliberately obtuse.

'About us. We have to look it in the eye some day. Might as well be now.'

'What about us?'

'There's nothing wrong with falling in love for a second time,' he said, steady and unhurried. 'You've just said so yourself. I still love Peg – always will, I tell you that now, straight, it wouldn't be right to pretend otherwise.'

'I know, Matt. I understand. But—'

'That doesn't mean I don't have it in me to love someone else.'

'Oh no! Of course not! You have the right to love and to be loved, Matt.'

'That's what I mean,' he said, eagerly. 'I think you need the same things, Alison. I think we could give each other a lot. I think maybe we—'

'But we're not the only people involved, Matt,' she interrupted.

'You mean Annie? She's not against me getting married again. I can tell you that for certain.'

'You've talked to her about this?' she said, startled. She hadn't thought he had got so far in his thinking.

'I haven't talked about it in so many words. But she . . . well, you know what Annie's like. She does a lot with actions, with being a help when you need it. She doesn't have to talk about things.'

'You think she'd accept someone else in Peggy's place?'

'I know she would.'

'But then . . . Matt . . . there's the twins.'

'What about the twins?' he said, genuinely surprised.

'If you marry again, you'll be choosing a new mother for the twins.'

'I know that!'

'You ought to be . . . very careful. It's for the rest of their lives.'

'You like 'em, don't you, Alison?' he asked, bewildered. 'I thought you took to them right off.'

'Oh, I did – they're lovely, adorable . . . It's just . . .'

'You mean you . . . you wouldn't want to take on a ready-made family?' His voice lost its steadiness. This was a stumbling block he hadn't envisaged.

'Oh, no – it's not that at all!'

'Then what?' He waited, and she could find no answer. 'You haven't anything against the idea of a second marriage?'

'No.'

'Then what is it?'

All at once she pushed away her hesitations, her scruples. The past was behind her, after all – as gone for ever as Matt's young wife.

'It's nothing. I'm just being silly. It's just that I never thought I'd ever want to get married again.'

'But you do?'

She nodded.

'Then that's all right, then!' He put his hands on her shoulders. 'We're – engaged?'

'Unofficially, yes. Let's keep it just between ourselves for a bit, Matt.'

'Yes, that might be best. I ought to speak to Annie first . . . I know that sounds funny but . . . I wouldn't want her to think I'm slighting Peggy.'

'I wouldn't want that either. And besides, I—'

'What?'

'Never mind. I'll tell you some time. I ought to give you more of an idea of what my life has been . . . But not now, Matt.'

'No, not now,' he said, and leaning forward kissed her very gently on the lips.

Next day, when he thought about that evening, Matt

couldn't be sure that it had all really happened. The idea that he could be happy again was new to him – not that he'd been unhappy in any vast, crippling way but he had had a sense of being lost for so long that to have a path mapped ahead was incredible.

He didn't want to talk to anyone about it. Not even to Annie. To talk about it might make it all disappear. For this reason he fell in with Alison's wish to keep their relationship to themselves for a time, as far as that was possible in the close-knit Beckindale community. He sensed that people were eyeing them, but no one actually asked if they had an understanding. In the main, the family at Emmerdale were too wrapped up in Joe's affairs to look too closely at Matt's.

Joe was having his problems. His prospective father-in-law refused to speak to him on the telephone, ignored letters, even paid no heed to the wedding invitation. There had been at least one quarrel with Christine, although Joe was by no means sure what it had been about. He was in the wrong, that was clear; he had apologized without quite knowing for what, and everything went back to being happy and loving again.

Then came a black day for Joe, a day he never confided to anyone. At market he happened on Christine's father and got talking to him on friendly terms. It was only after they had had a pleasant conversation about the livestock on sale that they introduced themselves. Joe, on learning the stranger's identity, had been ready for a fight.

But strangely enough Mr Sharp had been sad and quiet. He told Joe that the best thing he could do was break off the engagement. 'Christine builds up these fantasies,' he warned. 'At the moment you're part of the one she's engaged on – being the young farmer's bride, all rustic charm and roses round the door. Get out while you can, Joe. You're heading straight for disaster!'

You couldn't fight with a man who spoke in that tone of weary despair. Joe was shattered. All the way home he thought about it, and tried to make up his mind to speak to Christine about it. But when he saw her, so normal and happy and busy, he put it all out of his mind. It was just that vengeful father of hers, using whatever weapon he could lay his hands on.

Yet as the days went by, Christine's behaviour began to

worry them all. The wedding began to be the main thing in her life. They were all to get themselves up in Edwardian clothes to match a design she had thought of, based on the engagement ring that Joe had given her. They were to be driven to the church in a coach and pair. The reception was to be on a grand scale, with a catering firm to provide the wedding breakfast. Joe had another argument with her, more serious this time, about who was to pay for all this.

He never could remember afterwards quite how she talked her way out of that. He learned that she had money of her own, much more than he had. He remembered becoming very angry about that, very resentful, and being made to feel ashamed for what he said. Then she soothed and cajoled him, told him money didn't matter. And after all, it must be true, mustn't it? – because he had very little, and yet she was prepared to throw in her lot with him.

Even so, he worried about the things she was buying for their future home. She came back to Emmerdale with parcels and boxes: there was nowhere else to take them as yet, for they were still house-hunting. Only a few houses within Joe's price-range were available close enough to Emmerdale to make it possible for him to be there early and late. The obvious solution was to use Hawthorn Cottage.

Yet Joe couldn't bring himself to speak to Matt about Hawthorn. He knew how much it meant to him still. It held the ghost of Peggy, and the memory of the twins' birth, and their very first days at home as new parents – the days when Matt kept 'popping up to Hawthorn' from the fields for the mere pleasure of seeing them asleep, rosy fists curled against rounded cheeks; the nights when Matt would rise to listen, stooping anxiously over the cot to hear that soft, almost inaudible breathing.

Joe sensed that Christine wanted Hawthorn. It fitted in with her dream of an 'old-world' marriage and an 'old-world' home. The things she was buying were part of a decor she had in mind. When he asked her how they were to pay for these pewter coffee-pots and crewel-worked pictures, she waved the thought away. 'Oh, they'll send an account,' she said.

'But what happens when we can't pay t'bill?'

'They'll wait,' she said. 'They don't press . . .'

It was over Joe's affairs that Matt at last talked to Annie about his own. He was waiting to drive her and her father into Hotten: the old man was putting it off as long as he could, for he was to have his eyesight tested for the very first time, and was going only under protest. 'I don't need glasses!' he growled.

'Joe and Chrissie know they may have to do t'milking if we're delayed?' Annie asked Matt.

'Aye, they're in t'mistle now.'

She busied herself with putting a casserole ready in the oven for the evening meal, should she be late in coming back. Her back to Matt she said, 'Have they said anything to you about Hawthorn, Matt?'

'No, what about it?'

'Well, you know . . . they've looked at places, but there's nowhere, really.'

'I thought they'd move in here.'

'You mean with our having an extra room now Dry's nearly finished t'loft?' She closed the oven door and moved to the sink, where the potatoes waited to be taken from the bowl and put into a pot. 'I'm willing enough,' she said, 'but I think Christine would like a place of her own. It's only natural.'

'And she wants Hawthorn.' It wasn't a question. He had sensed it for some time. Now and again Christine would say things like, 'That colour would be just right for a cottage like Hawthorn ' or 'When I see a piece of furniture about the right date, I think how it would look in the living-room at Hawthorn.'

'I'm mentioning it because it's your house,' Annie said. 'We agreed that it should be yours for as long as you wanted.'

'Aye.' He knew he should say more, but his throat had closed up.

He was overwhelmed by the strength of his own emotion. He had somehow put a curtain between his memories of Hawthorn with Peggy and the twins, and what it would be like when he married Alison. He had shirked the idea of a new woman there in Peggy's place – not consciously, but he knew it now at Annie's words. It hurt so much to think of Christine there – what would it be like if he asked Alison to live with him there?

Peggy, with her shoulder-length hair held back by a shoelace, trying to hang a picture on the uneven walls of the living-room. Peggy, a folded towel over her shoulder, holding baby Sally against it as she rubbed her back and crooned to her after a feed. Peggy, out in the garden with the wind snatching at her flowered apron, pinning out the wash on the line . . .

Anne was watching him. She saw the shadows gathering on his face at the memories. 'Matt,' she began.

'Peg'll be dead a year next week,' he said. He put up a hand to his brow, the tips of his fingers touching his forehead as if he felt a stab of pain there.

With a swift movement Annie came to his side. 'I'm sorry, Matt . . .'

'We were happy there. And the twins . . .' His voice broke. 'Oh, Christ! Oh, Peg, Peg . . .'

His mother-in-law put her hand on his shoulder. She said not a word. She didn't even look at him as he bent his head and tried to hide his grief from the world.

It had been long in coming. When Peggy died he had said almost nothing. Others who didn't know him said, 'He's stunned. He can't take it in.' But Annie knew better. She was well aware that he didn't speak because he dared not. His silence, his withdrawal from the rest of the world – that had been his mourning. For a year now she had seen him going about his work much as usual: steady, reliable, good-tempered.

But he had been in misery and pain. She knew this because she herself had suffered in something the same way. She too was reticent. So she stood quietly by while Matt, for the first time, wept for Peg.

It took him a long time to recover from that moment. Although quite soon he appeared normal, and drove Sam and Annie into Hotten without attracting any sharp remarks from the old man, he was very quiet all day.

That night, in bed, he tried to come to terms with what had happened. He had been asked to face up to the idea of breaking once and for all with his past by giving up his home to Joe and Christine – and he had found he couldn't do it.

Now that was unfair. It was unfair on Joe and Christine, who needed a place to live. It was unfair on Alison, who held herself promised to him although nothing had been said to the world in general. He couldn't expect to make a new beginning with Alison if he let himself be held by invisible ties to the old life.

He loved Peggy. He had told Alison so. But that didn't mean he must be bound by the things that had belonged to Peggy. The cottage at Hawthorn, where they had lived briefly before she died, was after all only stones put together, slates for a roof, a neglected garden in front and a paddock at the back. It was a place to live, no more and no less.

And it might well be that Alison would want to live there once they were wed.

Before he could hand over the cottage to Joe, he had to find out whether Alison was ready to acknowledge publicly that they were engaged and, after that, whether she would like to be Mrs Matt Skilbeck of Hawthorn Cottage in the near future.

It took him a long time to come to this conclusion. He had a deep reluctance to cut off his memories of his pretty, lively Peggy. But in a way that had to be. He could go on loving her without having to live with the memory of her in every place he went to. Hawthorn ought to be used – and perhaps he and Alison were the right people to use it.

He had a date with Alison for next evening but, unfortunately, not alone. A friend from Liverpool, Louise Trowbridge, was staying overnight with Alison and Matt was invited to dinner to help entertain her. He was a bit nervous at the idea – he was never at his best with strangers.

However, Louise turned out to be a talkative, fun-loving woman who put him at his ease at once. Alison had made a special effort over the food and, as his part, Matt had asked Henry Wilks for advice on a bottle of wine which he had contributed. They had a merry meal, listening for the most part to Louise's tales of her life as a ship's stewardess.

'All you read in novels about life on shipboard is quite true,' she told Matt with a widening of her bright blue eyes.

'I've never read a novel,' Matt confessed. 'Except *Field of Tares*, but that was by my brother-in-law so I felt I had to. Didn't understand a word of it.'

'Your brother-in-law? Jack Sugden is your brother-in-law?'

'Aye, that famous author and failed farmer.'

'Good gracious!' The conversation turned at once on the

topic of Jack and his adventurous life. As a best-selling novelist, his actions had figured in the gossip columns. By and by Alison said she would do the washing up if Matt would take Louise over to the Woolpack for a liqueur to round off the evening.

'Nay, we'll wait—'

'No, I'll only be a minute. You can tell Louise about Jack. I've heard it all before!'

So he obeyed, taking their guest across the road to the warm companionship of the Woolpack where Jack had so often sought refuge. Louise asked for a gin and tonic, rather than a liqueur. Thankfully Matt bought himself a half of beer, and brought the drinks back.

After they had sipped in silence, Louise said, 'Matt, I'd like to tell you how grateful I am.'

'Grateful? What for?'

'For the way you—' She broke off. 'You do know about what she went through?'

'Oh aye.' He nodded. 'It gives us a sort of fellow-feeling.'

To his surprise, she looked up at him with a puzzled frown. 'Fellow-feeling? You?'

'Peggy, my wife . . . she died a year ago.'

'Oh yes.' Her face cleared. 'That would bring you two together, I see that. But I was thinking of all the rest of it.'

'What was the worst for her?' he asked, thinking of his own long sense of being lost, lost in the middle of a crowd.

'Oh, the way her so-called friends deserted her. It was bad enough at first, but after she came out—'

'Out?'

'That was the worst time. I think only myself and one other stuck by her. And that was just when she needed friends most, when she needed to fit herself back into society.'

'But Alison fits easily—'

'Oh, she has here, I can see that. She's been lucky, in a way. To have found a new friend like you, Matt, just when she needed one most, to give her the confidence to face life again . . .'

Matt was completely at a loss. 'She's found more than one friend here,' he said, searching for firm ground. 'Mr Ruskin—'

'Oh yes, he's a fine man. I admire him enormously. He believes in that bit from the Bible, I'm sure – "Let him that is without sin among you cast the first stone." But that's all behind Alison now, isn't it? And with your help she's making a fresh start.'

CHAPTER SIX

It was strange how life went on just as usual after that shattering conversation with Louise. Alison joined them, they talked away the evening, everything seemed normal. If Matt heard the chatter through a kind of haze, no one noticed.

Dry Hogben came in for his usual half. Amos greeted him with sour hospitality. He was waiting for the day when Dry would order something more than that, but from the way he seemed to refuse money for his work, he would never have enough in his pocket to pay for a pint.

'Evening, Alison,' Dry said, coming over to stand by their table. 'Matt . . .'

Alison introduced Louise. Louise looked interested, as who would not at this tall, bearded, musketeer-like figure. A sort of battle of wits ensued between the two, Louise laughing and teasing, Dry parrying all her thrusts.

'It's a pity I'm only staying till the morning,' she sighed. 'I'm sure I'd reduce you to order if I were here for a week or two.'

'Don't flatter yourself,' Alison said. 'We've all tried. He's not reducible.'

'I hope not. No sale price bargains, that's my attitude,' said Dry. 'My friends have to go shopping during ordinary price maintenance.'

'You talk very glibly about prices,' Louise said, 'but Alison tells me you don't know the value of money.'

'Ah? So she's been talking about me, has she? That's hopeful. And just for that, I'll buy you a drink. I do have some money,' he added as Alison raised her eyebrows. 'The Prescotts paid me for re-wiring their cottage.'

'You won't keep it if you spend it on us.'

'Cigarettes and whisky and wild wild women,' Dry said. 'Or at least the Beckindale equivalent . . . What will you have?'

After some argument and reluctance, they accepted his invitation. Matt went to the bar with him to fetch the drinks.

'You're not saying much,' Dry remarked as they watched Amos dispense the spirits.

'Haven't much to say.'

'Anything wrong?'

'Nay, what should be?'

'Very little, I'd think, for a man who's got such pleasant companions.'

Amos put the two shorts down on the bar. He was beaming. Dry had actually bought something more than half a pint. He turned to get the tonic for Louise's gin, then put the coke alongside the rum which Alison had asked for.

'Never used to serve much of this,' he remarked. 'I remember when Alison first came here and talked about rum-and-coke, I couldn't believe folk drank stuff like that.'

Matt hesitated. 'She came to work for you,' he said. 'Did she write to you asking for a job?'

Amos, now pulling beer, didn't hear the query. Dry, about to pick up the drinks, paused. He turned towards Matt, his penetrating eyes scanning his face.

'Are you going to marry Alison?' he asked.

Yesterday, if Matt had been asked that question, his answer would have been an unhesitating yes. Now he frowned. 'What's it to do with you?' he said.

'Oh, quite a lot. I talk to Alison, she talks to me.'

'What does she talk about?' Matt said. Strange though it might seem, Alison could have confided in Dry. He was the kind of person to whom you told things.

'The price of baked beans, mainly. She's a remarkable woman. I admire her.'

He waited. By all the rules of friendship, Matt should have said, 'I admire her too.'

Amos put the beer on the counter in front of him. To Dry he gleefully announced the cost and held out his hand. Dry said, 'This isn't going to start a habit, you know, Amos.'

'I'm thankful for small mercies,' said Amos. He took the pound note and went to the till.

'Amos is a wise man,' Dry remarked to Matt. 'Thankful for small mercies. We'd be happier if we were like that. Thankful for large mercies, too – because some of us are lucky enough to receive those.'

Matt looked at him. 'What are you saying?' he asked.

'I'm just pondering on the thought that I see a man who has a chance of happiness – great happiness. Yet he doesn't grab it.'

'I could say that I see a man who doesn't hold on to anything at all,' Matt countered.

'Touché. But then I don't want to hold on to things. You're different, Matt. You need to have strong, steady relationships.'

Matt looked down at the bar top. He found it difficult to talk about such things. Yet it was important – and after all, Dry was an outsider and it's said outsiders see most of the game.

'I need something else,' he murmured. 'I need to know that people are to be trusted.'

'Trusted? Trust is a two-way thing, Matt. Others have put their trust in you – and not been let down. Don't change now.'

'Change? How d'you mean, change?'

'Well, from where I stand, it looks as if you're more or less engaged to Alison and yet you shy away from making it public. I'd say Alison has trusted you with her affection—'

'But it was Alison who wanted it kept unofficial in the first place.'

'And you went along with it. But the good people of Beckindale are expecting more than that. You're not going to disappoint them, are you, Matt?'

Amos came back with Dry's change. 'Hey-up,' he remarked, 'those folk from Connelton are back. Asked after you, they did, Dry.'

Dry turned. An elderly man in a good dark suit and a very elegant young woman had come in at the door.

Matt never quite understood what happened next. All he knew was that Dry had gone. His untouched tankard of beer stood on the counter, his change lay where Amos had put it.

'Good heavens,' Amos said.

It was a fitting end to an evening that seemed full of confusion and distress. Matt was glad to say goodnight to Alison and her friend and head back for Emmerdale.

All night he tossed and turned. Louise's words kept echoing in his head. 'That's all behind Alison now, isn't it?'

What was behind Alison? What did it mean?

Now that he came to think about it, he knew nothing about her. She had come to Beckindale a little less than a year ago. He had first seen her in the Woolpack, where she had brought some much needed improvements, and she had quickly been on friendly terms with Henry Wilks. Henry had helped her to buy the village shop.

That was really all he knew except that she was a widow; she had mentioned her husband by name, and had let slip one or two hints as to his character. But that left a huge gap.

What was she doing in Beckindale in the first place? A pretty, intelligent woman like that? Why wasn't she in the city, where the chances were so much better? It wasn't even as if she was a devoted country-lover, like those who sell up everything to commune with nature. She went out for walks, true, and did some birdwatching with Henry – but she took no great part in local affairs, made no effort to have a garden in the yard behind the shop, was quite eager to go into Hotten or Leeds or Bradford for her day off.

Matt went to the Woolpack next day for a lunchtime drink. Amos was still marvelling over the lightning-like disappearance of Dry on the previous night.

'Never saw anybody move so fast! If they'd been police after him, he couldn't have run faster!'

'They've been up to t'farm,' Matt told him. 'They found out he was working for us.'

'Aye, I saw no harm in telling 'em that,' Amos defended himself. 'They'd been in a couple of times looking for him.' He waited, hoping to be told why they wanted Dry. When Matt said nothing he went on, 'Always said there was something funny about him. A man that only ever has enough to buy a half . . .'

'But you got some money out of him last night, Amos.'

'Oh, aye. Left his change. It's here, tell him, if he wants it.' Amos polished the counter. 'Friend of Alison's, I take it.'

'Who? Dry?' Matt was puzzled.

'No, the young lady. From Liverpool.'

'That's where Alison used to live, isn't it?'

'That's right.'

'Funny, ending up in a place like Beckindale.'

'How d'you mean, funny?' Amos was rather indignant. 'It may be smaller than Hotten and less posh than Connelton, but there's nowt wrong wi' Beckindale.'

'I only wondered how she ever came to hear of t'Woolpack. You advertised for staff, I suppose?'

'I don't recall,' Amos said, frowning at Matt. 'It's a long while ago.'

Matt drank some of his ale. This was proving much more difficult than he expected. The usually talkative Amos Brearley seemed very uncommunicative on this score. Moreover, Matt found it very distasteful to be fishing for information. It was a thing he'd never done in his life before.

That he had brought himself to do it was a proof of its importance to him.

Amos, for his part, had quickly become aware of what was happening. Matt wanted to know about Alison's past – and Amos had no intention of telling him, because in the first place he had promised the vicar never to tell a soul, and in the second he now liked and respected Alison Gibbons.

'What kind of qualifications do you put down when you advertise for a barmaid?' Matt inquired.

'Oh . . . experienced, reliable . . . that kind of thing.'

'You'd ask for references.'

'Not if I had personal recommendation.'

'Aye, that would make a difference.'

'I hired Mrs Gibbons and I never regretted it,' Amos said, on a sudden spurt of feeling. 'One of the best, she is.'

'I wondered how she came to know you had a job available.'

'She'd tell you if you asked her, I daresay.'

'Aye,' Matt said, and drained his glass.

Amos took the empty glass from him as he turned away. 'And don't forget to let me know if Dry Hogben's coming back for that change he left,' he added. 'Folk acting peculiar . . . don't know where I am . . .'

Matt might actually have remembered to give the message to Dry if he had seen him again, but Dry had gone. Not just from the Woolpack, nor from Emmerdale, but from the district. As the day went by it became clear he wasn't where he was expected to be – carrying out a fence-painting job for a farmer out Littlewell way. He had cleared out, leaving his tent still pitched up on the slopes above the farm and his few belongings within it.

The good-looking, elegant girl who had come into the Woolpack in search of Dry proved to be his fiancée, Celia Winterton. Between her and Christine, a friendship sprang up.

'It's nice for Christine to have someone in her own group to talk to about clothes and that,' Joe said to Matt as they worked in the barn the next day.

'She must find it hard from her side though – Celia, I mean. Helping Chrissie choose clothes for a wedding, when her own is postponed indefinitely.'

'It's a rum do,' Joe agreed, pausing with the feed fork in the air. 'Chris says he can't face responsibility. He's got an estate and a title waiting for him in the south – but he keeps disappearing.'

Matt nodded. 'He were offering me free advice the other night,' he said drily.

'Advice about what?'

'Oh, life in general. Marriage . . .'

'You and Alison, you mean?'

Matt looked away. 'Is it as obvious as all that?'

'We-ell . . .' Joe was troubled. 'I don't want to barge in, Matt. But 's'matter of fact, I ought to speak to you. About Hawthorn, you know.'

'It's only fair you should have it,' Matt said, stifling a sigh.

'You sure, Matt?' Joe stooped so he could look into the face of his brother-in-law. 'Won't you be wanting to move in there with Alison?'

'Nothing's settled. We haven't made any plans.' No, nor can we, Matt said within himself, until I know what's behind all this talk about Alison's past.

That there was something to know, he was now sure. His talk with Amos Brearley had proved that to him. Amos had been so determined not to gossip – it was so out of character.

So Amos knew. And perhaps the vicar knew. And Henry? Did Henry know?

It began to seem to Matt that everyone knew about Alison – except the man who wanted to marry her.

'Well, then, for t'time being, we'll take it we can move into Hawthorn,' Joe said awkwardly. 'But if ever you want it, it's yours – you know that.'

The talk at Emmerdale all that day was, as it had been on the previous day, about Dry Hogben. 'I can't understand a man behaving like that,' Christine said in a subdued tone. 'He practically left Celia at the church.'

'Nay, lass, it isn't as bad as that,' Sam said. Sam had developed a soft spot for Dry even though the younger man had borrowed his precious tools without permission.

'I couldn't live if a thing like that happened to me,' Christine replied.

'It's not likely to, so don't fret about it. In a way, happen what Dry's done is for the best. Marriage is a serious thing – if he's not sure it's right, he's best to clear off.'

'Without a word?' Christine objected.

'Well, that were wrong. He should have had an explanation, I suppose – aye, that would have been better.'

Matt listened in silence. It went home to him. When the meal was over that evening and the others had dispersed about their own interests, he said to Annie, 'You know you said to me you wouldn't mind a woman coming here in Peg's place?'

'I remember, Matt.' She took up her knitting. 'To tell the truth, I've been expecting more to come of that.'

'That friend of Alison's – the one I were asked to supper with.'

'Oh, aye?'

'She said . . . At least, didn't say – that's the trouble.'

'How can there be trouble from something she didn't say?'

'She . . . she seemed to take it for granted that I knew all about it.'

'About what?'

'That's what I don't know, Ma. She talked about Alison coming "out" of some place, as if she'd been ill or something. Did you ever hear of Alison having a nervous breakdown, or something serious – you know, TB or something?'

Annie's hands with their knitting were still. 'Nay, I've heard nothing of that sort. But then why should I?'

'It's a bit of a problem.'

'You mean, for you, or for her?'

Matt moved restlessly about the kitchen, the firelight glinting on his mop of blond hair. 'Look, I haven't got just myself to think about. There's t'twins . . .'

'That's true.' Annie had already gone through the dangers in her mind. If Matt married a woman who was subject to some serious illness, what kind of a mother was that for the bairns? They were little bundles of energy, too much of a handful really for Auntie Beattie. A sick woman could never deal with them. And it wouldn't be fair on them – or on Matt.

'But she seems so well, Matt,' she ventured.

'There's something, though,' he said, stopping to lean on the scrubbed table with his fists.

'Why don't you ask her?'

'How can I, Ma? "Did you ever have a nervous breakdown?" – you can't say that to anyone.'

'Seems to me Alison herself would know how important it is for the twins if there was anything like that to be told.'

'But whatever it is, she's never spoken about it. That can only be because she don't want to.'

'Happen it's because she can't, Matt.'

'Can't?'

'You couldn't talk about Peg – until lately.'

He was silent for a long moment. He sank down on a chair by the table.

'Aye,' he said at length. 'There's things that you can't talk about, and it don't have to be facts or events, it can be feelings. But this is a fact, Ma. Her friend Louise spoke of it, as something that had happened.'

'Then the only person who can set your mind at rest is Alison.'

Matt couldn't accept that. It was too final – to walk up to Alison and ask her outright. What if the reply proved to be something bad? Bad enough to make a difference to them?

And yet that could hardly be so. Alison didn't have the air of a woman with a guilty secret.

All the same, he stayed away from Beckindale. Where once he had taken every excuse to go into the village for Annie's errands, now he invented work to do that kept him busy – or, rather, he didn't invent work, for summer was upon them now and there was the hay to get in.

Joe was beginning to sound anxious about his own wedding. 'I can't seem to get Christine to understand what a bad time she's chosen for it,' he said. 'I don't want to be off in Portugal for two weeks during harvest.'

'Portugal?' Matt said, surprised into a laugh. 'I didn't know you were going to Portugal.'

'Oh, it changes from one day to t'next. Hungary, the Costa Brava . . . I think the favourite's Paris.'

'Paris would be nice,' Matt said, rather envious. 'Romantic, is that.'

'Garn,' Joe growled, thoroughly fed up. 'I can't even speak the language. I'd rather be somewhere a bit handier in case things go wrong here.'

'You don't want to think about Emmerdale while you're on your honeymoon, Joe.'

Joe suddenly shrugged in defeat. 'I just don't know where the money's going to come from for all this, and that's a fact, Matt. Henry put it to me a while ago – the bride's family should pay for wedding and all that, by rights. But we can't even get a word out of Christine's dad.'

'So it's all down to us, is it?'

'Seems like it. I don't like to see Ma with so much on her shoulders. The whole thing's grown so . . . so unmanageable.'

'Aye,' Matt sighed, 'things kind of get away from you, don't they . . .'

He couldn't bear his own inaction any longer. He would make one more try to find out what lay in Alison's past, by approaching someone whom he suspected of knowing it all. He went to see Edward Ruskin, vicar of Beckindale.

Ruskin was a quiet, farsighted man who respected Matt although Matt was not a churchgoer. He was surprised when he was announced, and almost at once suspected the reason for his visit.

'Will you have a cup of coffee with me?' he invited. 'My wife's just brought this in.'

'Well . . . thank you, vicar . . . only I don't want to take up your time.'

'Why shouldn't you? You very seldom make any claims on me, Mr Skilbeck.'

'Last time was over the christening.'

'Yes, and I hope the twins are flourishing.'

'They're fine, thanks.' Matt floundered for a moment. 'It was Mrs Gibbons who talked me into having them baptized.'

'Was it? That doesn't surprise me. She's always been a convinced Christian in her own quiet way.'

'You've known her a long time, vicar?'

'Yes, several years.'

'Since her Liverpool days?'

'Quite right.'

'I've wondered why she came to Beckindale, in the first place.'

'She came because I suggested it, Mr Skilbeck.'

'Why was that?'

'I thought she would be happy here.'

'Happier than before?' Matt said. 'She'd had . . . troubles?'

'Don't we all,' sighed Mr Ruskin.

'She doesn't talk about them much,' Matt said, colouring at his own duplicity, for the fact was that Alison didn't speak of them at all – to him.

'She talks about them to people she chooses to confide in,' the vicar said gently. 'And that, of course, is a great compliment. One that can't be negated by making them a topic of casual conversation.'

'I'm not being casual,' Matt replied. 'It's serious for me, vicar. Alison and I have talked about getting engaged.'

'That's splendid. When you get to the point of marriage, I hope it will be in church, Mr Skilbeck.'

Skilfully deflected, Matt's intended inquiries died on his lips. He stayed a few minutes longer then left, no wiser than when he had come – except that he felt sure that when the vicar spoke of friends in whom Alison had confided, that included Henry Wilks.

Henry was out with his binoculars watching the birds rise up ahead of the haymaking machines. Quite by chance Matt came upon him on the slope of Blea Head, where he had gone in search of peace and quiet to think.

'Hello, you not out on the tractor?' Henry greeted him.

'Nay, Joe's on this morning. I'm taking over this afternoon.'

'Anything wrong, Matt?'

All at once Matt came right out with it. 'Tell me about Alison,' he said. 'I've a right to know.'

Henry was taken aback. This man was his rival – his successful rival for Alison's hand. He had taken it for granted that Alison had told him everything, just as she had told Henry himself when he proposed. The fact that Matt was still in the dark could mean only one thing: they weren't as close to each other as Henry had thought.

'I can't talk to you about Alison's affairs,' he countered. 'You should know that, Matt.'

'You mean she's told you?'

'Well . . . it was a while ago. There was a reason.'

'Why hasn't she told me?' Matt cried. 'I don't understand!'

Henry put his binoculars into their case. 'You have to realize that unhappiness leaves a scar, Matt. Good lord, I shouldn't need to tell you that, after what you went through when Peg died.'

'But that's it,' Matt pointed out. 'I don't keep it a secret that Peg died. Why won't Alison speak about what happened?'

'I suppose it's because there's still an emotional block. That can happen, Matt. The human mind is a funny thing. It can make us do things we don't really want to do – it makes us punish ourselves for crimes we haven't actually committed. Alison is still suffering from some kind of aftermath, I think.'

'You mean she was mentally ill?'

'No, no – emotionally ill is more the right term. That husband of hers . . . Ah well, we shan't speak ill of the dead. But you can take it from me that the bad time in Alison's life was due to the way her marriage was going. She'll tell you herself one day, when's she's ready. Until then I shouldn't worry your head too much about it. It doesn't worry me, and I know the story – so you see it isn't important except for the fact that Alison can't forgive herself for something that she was driven to by unhappiness.'

To show that he had said all he intended to, Henry glanced at his watch. 'Time for lunch,' he said. 'Come to the Woolpack and I'll buy you a drink, Matt.'

'No thanks. I'm expected back at Emmerdale. Joe's waiting for me.'

Matt went down the dale with a lightened step that matched his lightened heart. What he had gleaned from Henry had been reassuring. Alison had been made unhappy by her husband, and there had been some crisis. Friends had turned their back on her. Mr Ruskin had come to her aid and invited her to Beckindale. It might all have been a health thing, after all.

They were very busy at the farm for the next few days. If he had been looking for an excuse to stay away from Alison, he had it now, what with Joe trying to clear a space in the next few weeks to go away on his honeymoon with a clear conscience, and the hay to come in, and the early grain crops ripening ahead of time in the hot summer.

He could have rung her, of course. But Matt wasn't good with the telephone. And besides, it was difficult to be alone long enough to say anything worth saying on the phone in the farm kitchen. So he left it, hoping that Alison would understand.

At length came an evening when the pressure had eased. He set out for Beckindale to see her, almost looking forward to the explanation he had dreaded so long. He would ask her what had happened in her past, and she would tell him, and it would all prove to be nothing. Then he would ask her to name the day.

CHAPTER SEVEN

Alison had closed up thankfully that day. It was hot and dry in the village; people had been coming all day for tins of bitter lemon and coke. Now she was happy to be in her cool little kitchen, that faced north over the moors, and making herself a strong cup of tea.

She came down at the knock on the shop door. Some farmer's wife needing extra supplies to feed the harvesters – you couldn't refuse to open to them.

She fell back at sight of Matt. 'Hello! Fancy seeing you,' she said in laughing accusation. 'If it hadn't been for Annie coming in for the groceries, I'd have thought all of you at Emmerdale had died and gone to heaven.'

'Well, you know how it is,' Matt said, embarrassed. 'What with the work, and Joe's wedding, and Dry disappearing and us having his folk round us . . .'

'Come and have a cup of tea. I'm just making it.'

He followed her, anxiously clutching the small box of expensive chocolates that Christine had bought for him on her last shopping trip to Harrogate.

'I should have written a thank-you note for that meal you gave me,' he said.

'Nonsense, it was I who should have said thank you to you for helping to entertain Louise.'

'Well, anyway, this is a kind of peace offering.' He held out the package.

'Oh, Matt! How nice of you! Oh, what lovely chocolates! Hand-made – oh, heavens, they're irresistible, I must open them.'

She did so, and beamed with pleasure at the sight of the sweets each in its separate nest of white foil. 'Now I'm not going to eat one,' she said, 'not till I've had my meal . . . I'll have a cup of tea instead, to keep my mouth from watering.'

She poured the tea, offering his cup to Matt. 'Sit down. It's nice to see you again.'

'I really have been busy, Alison.'

'I know. It's a busy time.'

He put down his cup with something of a clatter. 'Louise happened to say to me . . .'

'What?' She started, so that she spilled some tea into the saucer. 'Louise said – what?'

'She mentioned that you'd had a bad time. I was a bit—'

'Oh,' Alison said, her eyes widening. 'So that's why I haven't seen you.'

'I were a bit puzzled, like, but now I see it was silly to get in a state. It weren't your fault. You couldn't help it.'

'Is that what she said?'

'Nay she didn't say anything – but Henry thinks—'

'Have you been discussing me with everybody in Beckindale?' she asked.

'Of course not. It's only that I . . . I didn't like to come to you.'

'No?'

'For fear it distressed you.'

Very slowly, as if she were walking in her sleep, she went to the kitchen sink and emptied her tea into it. She put the cup and saucer down. Then she turned to Matt.

'What, actually, do you know?'

'Well . . . nothing, really . . .'

'But you want to know?'

A moment ago he would have said yes. But as he looked at the tension and misery in her face he changed his mind. 'No, Alison, it doesn't matter—'

'But it does, Matt. You have a right to know. It's not fair not to tell you.'

She still hesitated, however. Matt said, 'You've already told Henry?'

'A little. Mr Ruskin knows. Dry Hogben guessed at least some of it. So you must hear the whole thing. I have to go back a bit, Matt. To my marriage. You remember, I didn't really want to get married.'

'But you did.'

'Yes. It worried me that my parents disapproved, and then Peter – well, he began to be career-hungry, and he found when he applied for high-level jobs that they preferred a married man. Top executives have to have wives who can entertain, who can make the house look nice, who can turn up at office cocktail parties and be decorative. So we got married. In a church. A white wedding.'

'Yes, you told me . . .'

'I was a pretty bride. The sun shone. Everything should have been marvellous from then on. And for a while it was, it really was. But then I had a baby – a little girl. That was where it began to go wrong.'

'I don't see how—'

'Jennifer was a delicate baby. They did tests after a bit and discovered she had allergies to things – wool, dust, all kinds of things. At first I didn't know what I was doing wrong. It worried me, I was always tense and worried. The doctor used to say if I could only relax things would be better, but it's easy to say that when you're not in charge of a little scrap that's wheezing its life away . . .'

'That's terrible,' Matt said, thinking of his own two hearty little demons. 'I'm sorry, Alison.'

'I was always having to take her to hospital for some new treatment. Or if we had the top brass to dinner, I'd leap up in the middle of their best funny stories, to see if Jennifer was all right. I was a bore, a nuisance. And I didn't like to leave her to go to a party. I didn't trust her with a baby sitter. I was sure I'd get back from a party and find her wheezing to death. It's difficult for a man to understand . . .'

'But it isn't!' Matt protested. 'I see what you felt—'

She sighed. 'Well, Peter didn't. He'd go to a cocktail party on his own, and come back about eleven o'clock all happy and delighted, and want me to fall in with how he felt. But I'd be anxious and lonely and clinging . . . I handled it all wrong. I was a fool. I knew I was – but I couldn't seem to stop. So by and by Peter stopped coming home from cocktail parties straight away. He'd go on somewhere else with friends. Or *a* friend!'

Matt didn't know what to say. It was a life-style totally beyond his ken. He sat staring in helpless concern at Alison.

'I can see Peter's point of view,' she said in a strained, reasonable voice. 'I was no help to him in his career. In fact, quite the opposite. I was a drag. I thought more of the baby than I did of him, it must have seemed. He found consolation elsewhere . . .'

'Nay, don't say any more, Alison,' Matt said. 'You're only making yourself unhappy.'

'No, I want you to know it all. I haven't come to the really important bit yet. That began with the divorce.'

'Divorce?' He heard the shock in his own voice. 'But I thought you were a widow?'

'Wait,' she said. 'Peter asked me to divorce him. Of course there were grounds. I didn't want to, I held out against it. I knew of other women who'd lived through their husband's affairs . . . But I only drove him further and further away. In the end I said, "Yes, all right, whatever you say." But I never really wanted it, though I set the machinery in motion. It's quite a straightforward thing, you know, Matt. I'm told it can be quite painless.'

'I don't know,' he said helplessly. 'I never talked about it before.'

'When the decree nisi was given, I walked out of the court and went straight into a supermarket. I picked up half a dozen things and went out of the door without paying. I was arrested. I wanted to be arrested, I suppose. I was arrested and charged with theft.'

'Alison!'

'Does that shock you? Theft . . . that's what it is, after all. We give it a funny name but it's taking things that don't belong to you. My case came up before a magistrate who had just about come to the end of his patience with women like me. My lawyer – I had a lawyer, Peter insisted . . . My lawyer made a good case for me and I think I might have got probation, but I kept saying I'd do it again. I was a headline in the local paper "I'll go straight out and do it again, says shoplifter" . . . It was to punish Peter, of course. The people he worked for could forgive, could even applaud, adultery. But having a wife who went shoplifting – that wasn't so chic. They didn't enjoy that.'

'Alison, don't you think you misjudge your own state of mind—'

'I went to prison for six months,' she went on inexorably. 'Remission for good behaviour, of course. But even the short time I was in jail was too long. Peter had had to take charge of Jennifer – to do him justice, he rallied round quite well. He moved back into the flat, didn't see the other woman very much . . . At least, so I was told afterwards. But you see, Matt, he wasn't much good at looking after a baby, or even himself . . . He was terribly undomesticated. Somehow he managed to do something silly to the central heating boiler one cold night, and the fumes . . . the fumes . . . suffocated . . .'

'Alison!' Matt jumped up and came to her, to put his arms around her, but she eluded him.

'So you see, I am a widow,' she said in a voice that cracked with pain. 'Peter died, and so did Jennifer. And it was my fault. If I'd been there it would never have happened. If I'd stayed out of jail, Peter wouldn't have been looking after my baby. He'd have been with Frances, at her place in Chester. I brought it all about because I went out of my head one afternoon and took an armful of things that didn't belong to me out of a shop. And I only did that to get my own back on Peter.'

For a moment no one said anything. Alison picked up the teapot. 'This tea's cold,' she said. 'I'll make some more.'

'Nay, don't, Alison—'

'I want some,' she said. 'I don't think I drank the first lot.'

'Let me do it—'

'I can manage.' She put the kettle on the boiling ring and turned on the gas. The gas made a faint roaring sound. The kettle began to steam almost at once. She put tea in the pot and poured on the boiling water. She came back to the table with the teapot and sat down.

'I've imagined myself telling you all this,' she said. 'I've even thought of how to do it. It's come out all different.'

'That's because you're upset—'

'No,' she said heavily, 'it's because in my imagination I came to you and volunteered all the information. The difference in real life is that you had to ask me.'

'But that doesn't matter—'

'Yes it does. It changes things. It demonstrates to you that I still haven't got over it because I couldn't bring myself to tell you without being cornered. And it's all so much worse than you expected to hear, isn't it?'

He tried to choose his words. 'I'll not deny it's come as a shock—'

'Oh yes! Divorce! Theft! You've never spoken to anyone before in your life who has one of those to her credit, let alone both!'

'Alison, don't get angry with me,' he pleaded. 'I . . . I want to understand it all. It's just that I can hardly get my breath to speak.'

'Oh, don't bother!' she cried. 'You can't accept it – and why should you? I knew it would be like this! That's why I didn't want you to know! It's spoiled everything!'

'No, it needn't—'

'I think you'd better go,' she said. 'I can't bear it any more.'

'Alison—'

'Please go!'

Baffled and confused, he turned to the door. 'I'll come back tomorrow,' he muttered.

'No, don't. I don't think we'd better see each other any more.'

'But I—'

'Let's forget the whole thing, Matt.'

He shook his head helplessly and went out. Only after the door had closed on him did she see that he had brushed the little box of chocolates off the table so that they had scattered on the floor.

In a flood of tears, she knelt to pick them up. But they were bruised and tarnished, fit only for the rubbish bin.

Matt was home earlier than Annie had expected. She'd somehow got the feeling that this evening was to be a special occasion, with the box of chocolates as a good beginning. But when he came in about nine o'clock he seemed much as usual, and explained his actions by saying he had to get early to bed in preparation for another long day tomorrow.

But though he seemed his normal self, he was beset with emotions he had never had to deal with before. He was ashamed of himself, because it was true what Alison said – her confession had shocked him. He had gone to her home expecting to have an explanation but he had deceived himself into thinking it would all turn out to be something simple, innocuous. To find that she had lived through such a long, destructive emotional storm had stunned him.

He had no idea how he should have responded. All he knew was that he'd failed her – and himself.

The trouble was that he didn't know, he really didn't know, what to do next. She seemed a different person now, the Alison he'd thought he knew. That woman spilling out her story to him last night – that was a stranger. What should he do for the best? How should he approach her? When he saw her again, would she seem a stranger still – or would the old Alison, the Alison he loved, have come back?

Preoccupied with his own troubles, he went about the daily round at the farm, unnoticed. Annie had her hands full with the meals for the local harvesting groups. Sam was busy in his vegetable plot, where his prize potatoes were being nursed for the horticultural show. Joe and Christine were, as ever, preoccupied with their forthcoming wedding.

That afternoon Christine sought an opportunity to talk to Matt. From her point of view, there was something very important and urgent to settle – the disposal of the pieces of furniture at Hawthorn Cottage that belonged to Matt.

'You see, Matt,' she began, 'Joe and I have got things of our own we want brought in . . .'

'Brought in where?'

'At Hawthorn,' she said, wishing he would pay attention. 'In a way, it's a pity to have your things crammed into a little room there. That's the way things get damaged.'

'Crammed?' Matt said vaguely. He was roaming the kitchen, looking for something to have with his afternoon tea. 'Where are you going to cram them?'

'In what will eventually be the guest room . . .' She busied herself with making the tea, conscious she was a little behind schedule because Annie, before she left to buy herself a wedding hat in Leeds, had told her to put tea on the table by four o'clock.

'Aren't you going to use the things?' Matt inquired. 'I'd have thought you might as well have the use of them so long as you're there.'

Christine explained that with the things she and Joe had bought, there wouldn't be room for his furniture as well. As the conversation progressed, it dawned on Matt that Christine wanted the things out because she thought them poor stuff.

Matt had no idea whether the three piece suite and the mirror were good or bad – all he knew was that Peggy had chosen them, and what had been good enough for Peggy ought to be good enough for Joe's wife.

He told her in a clipped tone that he would see to the things. She offered to pay if he would put them in store. All at once Matt found himself resenting her manner. He could scarcely believe it as he felt his own temper rising. Not since he was a little boy had he been aware of a desire to hit out at someone.

'Of course there's things to be settled about Hawthorn besides my furniture,' he said.

'Such as what?'

'Such as . . . well . . . Peg and me . . .' He paused. He didn't want to be vindictive. But she was taking an awful lot for granted, all the same. 'The family's never sat down round a table and worked out what to do about Hawthorn,' he said.

'What is there to work out?' she asked, alarmed. 'It's all settled, surely. Joe and I are to have it.'

'For the time being.'

'What?'

'We signed an agreement eighteen months gone. I was to have Hawthorn as long as I wanted it.'

'But Joe said . . .'

'Joe said that you could move in. Fair enough. But we've never had a thorough discussion. I never said I was giving up Hawthorn for good.'

Christine's face went cold and stubborn. 'Have you said any of this to Joe?'

'It's never come up so far.'

'I think he ought to be told.'

'I'll tell him next time I see him.'

'I'll go and find him,' she said, and stalked out.

Matt sat where he was at the kitchen table, appalled at what had just happened. He had quarrelled with Joe's bride-to-be. What was happening to him these days? He was changing, he was being pushed into things he didn't understand, he seemed to have no control over what happened.

He got up and went out to the Landrover. Enough was enough. He was going to have it out with Alison no matter what she said about not seeing each other again.

His life was bound up with Alison's now. He couldn't stand back any longer and let Christine take over Hawthorn as if no one else had any claim to it. By rights the place was Matt's – and he might very well want it for himself before the year was out.

He drove down to the village rather faster than was his style. He found Alison standing in the customer part of the shop, pointing out things to Mrs Dawkins, a bossy and loquacious lady who sometimes acted as stand-in when Alison needed a day off. 'Are you sure you understand about the stand-by stocks?' Alison was asking as he came in.

'Eeh, lass, just you go off and leave it to me. Put it all out of your head.'

'Going away?' Matt asked, his heart giving a sudden lurch.

Alison turned. Her faced changed – seemed about to smile and then froze.

'I'm planning to have a holiday,' she said.

'Oh? That's a bit sudden, isn't it?'

'Not particularly. I usually go away towards the beginning of July.'

Matt moved uneasily from one foot to the other. 'Could I have a word?' he murmured.

'I'm rather busy, Matt.'

'It's important, Alison.'

'You go,' Mrs Dawkins urged. 'I'm here, you know. I'll see to everything.'

'But Mrs Dawkins, you don't know where—'

'I'll find everything. If anybody wants something I can't find, they can come back when you're here. Go on, you're only young once, luv.'

Thus exhorted, Alison allowed herself to be guided out into the High Street by Matt. He offered his arm. She took it. They walked out of the village towards the river.

From up on the slopes they could hear the combine-harvesters at work. The village was unusually empty; even the old men who sat on the bench by the green had gone to help bring in the crops.

'You wanted to speak to me?' Alison prompted in a cool tone.

'Aye. Christine has just been having a word wi' me about her plans for Hawthorn, and I thought ... I thought ... it was about time that you and I had a proper talk.'

'I thought we had that last night,' she said, very dry.

'That were more an outburst than a talk,' he said, with quiet humour. 'I got swept away by that, Alison. I didn't know where I was ...'

'That was fairly obvious.'

'Be fair, Alison,' he begged. 'You know yourself you'd have been a bit taken aback if I'd told you a story like that.'

To her own surprise she turned and smiled at him. The idea of Matt having to make such a torturous confession was absurd.

'I'm sorry,' she said. 'I was unreasonable to expect you to take it all without turning a hair.'

'And I was unsympathetic to be so much at a loss.'

'Unsympathetic? You? Never. Quite the contrary. You were bowled over by pity. I could see that.'

'Well, I ...' He was uncomfortable. He pressed on, 'Listen, Alison, it's come to a moment when we've got to make up our minds what we really want to do.'

'We?'

'Joe and Chris, you and me.'

She looked at him, waiting.

'It's my fault, I think. I went along with the way things were going. Joe and Chris want to move into Hawthorn. It seemed only logical. I didn't care then – at least, not so much.'

'And now?' she queried.

'It's different now,' he said. 'You and I have got to know each other pretty well, and then after last night ... You see, Alison, I feel that now I'm involved ... is that the word? Involved? I've a part to play in your life, that's what I mean. I could happen make things good for you again.'

She leaned on the parapet of the bridge and looked at the reflection of the westering sun on the river. After a moment she shook her head without speaking.

'Alison?' he insisted.

'No,' she said.

'What?'

'No, Matt.'

'But I thought ... After last night ...'

'What about last night?'

'Well, you and I know each other better than any other two people . . .'

'No. You're wrong. I told you what you had to know, because the time had come when I couldn't keep it from you any longer. But it doesn't mean we know each other better. It doesn't make us the perfect partners for each other. You've had unhappiness in your life, I've had it in mine. But that's no basis for a marriage, Matt.'

'But we like each other, Alison.'

'Oh yes. But it isn't love, Matt.'

'How can you be so sure? I don't know that I would care to speak with so much assurance, Alison . . . I mean, I really believe—'

'No, you don't, Matt. You loved Peggy. But can you really say you feel about me as you did about her?'

He stiffened. 'That's not fair, Alison. That were different. First time for both of us.'

'And now would it be second time, second best? Would it even be that? I saw your face last night, Matt dear. You were sorry for me, overwhelmed with pity for me, anxious to alleviate my pain, sorry that you'd ever made me relive those times – but I didn't see love.'

'Happen you had too many tears in your eyes, luv.'

She gave him a glance of muted admiration. 'You're quicker than you let on, Matt . . . But the answer's no. I can't try again. I'm not ready yet. That's why I'm going away on this holiday. I want a chance to think over what's happened, to see what I've learned – if anything. It wouldn't be right to start out on a marriage while I still didn't know whether I'd sorted myself out.'

He was about to argue, but she raised a hand and put her finger on his lips.

'I must get back,' she said. 'Mrs Dawkins will have put everything in a complete muddle if I stay away.'

Without allowing him time for another word, she turned and walked away.

Matt made no conscious decision to go to Hawthorn. He found the key in its usual hiding-place, opened the door, and walked in.

The first time since just after Peggy's funeral.

Everything looked strange, the way a place does when you've been away for a long time. It seemed smaller. He stood just inside the door of the living-room, staring at it. Had he really worked all hours of the day and night for a fortnight, to paper these walls and paint these doors so that he and Peg could move in when the twins were born? Had he really clambered up and down ladders putting up curtain rails, fixing shelves . . ?

He remembered the argument he had had with Peggy about the wallpaper. Well, not argument really, because Matt just never argued with Peggy. But he'd held out against her choice of paper on the grounds that the big, wandering pattern would make it difficult to match the joins and expensive because of wastage while matching; and in the end, by a kind of unconscious delaying tactic, he won the battle because the paper was all sold out when he got to the shop in Hotten at last.

So they had fallen back on Peg's second choice, this pale paper with a sort of fern design. Nice, really. He still liked it. Suitable, that was what it was. He moved to the wall opposite the window and studied his handiwork. Aye, not bad, that . . . You couldn't see the butt-marks.

Peg had said to him, 'You see, Matt? You can turn your hand to anything! You oughtn't to go on as if you were fit only for farm labouring. You could earn good money as a decorator.'

'But I like farm labouring. And 'sides, now Henry's come along with all these plans for Emmerdale, prospects there are good.'

Yes, since Henry came, everything had been different. Emmerdale was on a real business footing, Joe taking charge as if to the manner born, finding funds and time for Matt to specialize in sheep-breeding . . .

But Peg wasn't here to see it all. What was the point of it? Matt felt that he was to some extent a success – he more than pulled his weight at Emmerdale, he had won a prize last year with his ewes at a local show, his wages thanks to Joe were now more than adequate, his advice was listened to and respected not only at the farm but in the district. But what good was it?

He had thought he might share it with Alison. Despite all the obstacles that had arisen between them, he had felt that in the end she would come to him. The dreadful story she had told him about her past had shaken him – oh, he didn't deny that, but it hadn't altered his fundamental feeling that she was meant for him. He had been sure she felt the same, that once the shock of that interview was behind them she would hold out her hand to him.

A complete refusal . . . He hadn't expected that. He'd thought she might say, 'I need time. We mustn't rush it.' That would have been all right. He was a patient man – he wouldn't have minded waiting. He had waited a long time already for a happiness that seemed always to elude him – another few months wouldn't have mattered.

He could have gone to Joe and said, 'Look, it's okay for you and Christine to have Hawthorn for the half-year, while you look round for somewhere else.' In fact, Matt's brain had already worked it out that once he and Alison were wed and settled in Hawthorn, that would leave Matt's room at Emmerdale and, with the new room in the attic, ample space for the young couple to make their home at the farm. After all, it made sense. Joe would inherit one day; he might as well settle early in his married life into the farmhouse where he would live out his years.

Christine wasn't keen on that. Instinctively Matt understood this. Christine wouldn't mind being in total command of Emmerdale – with full powers to redecorate and refit it according to her taste. But, much though Christine respected Annie, she didn't want to live in the same house with her. That was only natural. Two women in one kitchen – it was a music-hall recipe for disaster. Oh yes, it was only natural that Christine would want to live elsewhere until the sad day came when Emmerdale belonged to Joe entirely.

And so she had wanted Hawthorn. Matt looked at the boxes and cartons stacked in the middle of the living-room; she'd collected a good few things for the new home already. Matt's furniture had been pushed against the wall to make way for the boxes; he walked to the collection and glanced at the contents of the nearest box – folded curtains, waiting to be hung. Rich, thick fabric, far better than those Peggy had made.

Their three-piece suite was lined up under the window. Uncut moquette – Matt had never understood what that meant. 'What's cut moquette, then?' he asked Peggy – but she'd only laughed and told him that this was a good upholstery fabric, strong and durable. He looked at the armchairs; they still had lace head-rests on the back to protect the uncut moquette from getting soiled where people leaned back.

Matt looked at them, and he suddenly knew that from Christine's viewpoint they were gimcrack, inferior, not at all the kind of thing she wanted cluttering up her home. All at once he was seized with a surge of ferocious energy. He picked up the nearest armchair and humped it up on to his back. He stalked through the door and out to the Landrover. A quick heave put the armchair in the back. He turned and hurried back for the second armchair. The settee was more difficult, but by turning it end over end he got it out in two or three minutes.

Now that he had started he wanted to finish it all quickly. He couldn't explain why he had this sudden urge to be over with it. It was as if a door was closing on his past life and he wanted to help to slam it – and by doing so acknowledge once and for all that it was over, and the future too. The future that was to have been based on this past, on Hawthorn and the chance of a happy family life with Alison and the twins – well, it wasn't going to happen. He would take his few things from Hawthorn and be done with it. Why not? Why cling on to foolish dreams? Why stand between Christine and her plans for a pretty home? Why behave as if he himself might want the cottage when it was clear that he was destined to be alone?

When he got back to Emmerdale, Christine was washing up after the evening meal. Annie still wasn't back from her jaunt to Leeds, but the others were sitting about the kitchen in that state of indolence that comes after a good tuck-in. Sam looked up as Matt came in.

'You missed a real good casserole,' he said with a nod towards Christine in acknowledgment of her cooking.

'Sorry I'm late,' Matt said.

'I kept yours for you,' Christine said. 'It'll be a bit dried up by now but not bad . . .' She smiled at him hesitantly. He could tell she was uncertain how to speak to him after their encounter earlier.

'I've been up to Hawthorn,' Matt said. 'I've cleared out my things.'

Joe, on the phone about some business matter, hung up with

a click. 'What did you want to do that for?' he said, looking appalled.

Matt shrugged. He was silent a moment as Christine served his food. Then, innately unwilling to cause any unpleasantness, he explained in a few gruff words that he had thought it best for everyone. Joe couldn't talk about it after a minute; he went upstairs to change for his evening out with Christine. He was still up there buttoning his shirt when he heard Matt come up after finishing his meal. He went out on the landing.

'Matt . . .' he said.

His brother-in-law halted on the dim staircase.

'Matt, you shouldn't have done that without talking it over first.'

'Ah well . . . I didn't see how talking would help.'

'But I mean . . . I know what it must have cost you, Matt.'

'Nay, it cost only a bit of energy—'

'I'm not talking about that, and you know it. It just seems wrong, somehow. Christine told me she'd spoken to you earlier this afternoon and got the impression that . . . that you wanted to hang on to Hawthorn. She and I had a bit of an argument, really. I told her she shouldn't have . . .'

'But she was right. My things were in her way.'

'But the place is *yours*, Matt. And if you feel you might want to move back there . . . you know what I mean . . .'

In the half-light of the landing it was impossible for Joe to see Matt's face, and for this Matt was thankful. Standing here outside the door of the bedroom he had shared with Peggy, and speaking of the house where he had hoped to live out his life with her, he couldn't control his facial muscles. He said nothing, and Joe waited.

At last Matt said, 'Don't you worry your head about me, Joe. I've come to terms with myself.'

'But what about . . . I mean, stop me if I'm wrong, Matt, but I reckoned you and Alison . . .?'

'Nay, that were a mistake. Seems I got the wrong idea somehow.'

'But you didn't!' Joe cried. 'I mean, anybody could see she—'

'No, that was only how it looked,' Matt said. 'It's easy to be wrong about how things look. I spoke to Alison and I discovered the look of the things was misleading because, you see, it's more mixed up than you think it is. There's more to things . . . complex, that's the word. They're more complex than you imagine. And any road, the long and short of it is that I'm not likely to want Hawthorn.'

Joe muttered something under his breath that Matt didn't quite catch. It was actually, 'Well, I reckon she's daft, then.' Aloud he said, 'It still seems wrong to me, Matt. To be building our happiness on . . . well, on your unhappiness.'

Matt managed a laugh. 'Don't start thinking like that, lad, or you'll never move a muscle for the rest of your life. Nay, don't you think like that about it. You've got your future to think of, you've got Christine – you look ahead, not behind or to the side. You get Hawthorn fitted up so Christine will be happy there.'

'And you really don't mind?'

'Go on downstairs,' Matt said. 'She's waiting for you.' For he found he couldn't reply directly and with truth, 'No, I don't mind.'

CHAPTER EIGHT

From that evening onwards, an irresistible tide seemed to sweep them all along towards Joe's wedding day. Joe himself confided to Matt that he didn't understand what was happening half the time. 'A good thing Ma and Chrissie are well-up on this wedding stuff,' he laughed. 'Best man, matron-of-honour – I don't know what on earth they're on about half the time.'

'What're you doing about t'best man?' Matt inquired, pausing as he was about to mount the tractor.

'Eh . . . well . . . I need to talk to you about that, Matt.' Joe, red in the face from exertion in the field and from embarrassment, stared up at Matt. 'I wrote to Jack, you know . . . asked him if he'd come back from Rome to stand in for me . . .'

'And what did he reply?'

'He hasn't written yet. What I was wondering, Matt . . . would you be best man if Jack says no?'

'Why not?' Matt replied. He leaned down and slapped Joe on the shoulder. 'We'll get you to the church on time, don't worry.'

When he heard that he would have to get himself up in a dress suit, he was less hearty about it. He muttered to Joe that he thought he would look a fool.

'How d'you think I feel?' Joe returned. 'I could strangle Ma for agreeing with Christine about this daft idea . . . but there you are. Ma says it's Chrissie's day and we must have it the way she wants it.'

The way Christine wanted it included a professional caterer who – to do him justice – worked wonders on the farmyard at Emmerdale for the reception. Alison was matron of honour in a very simple dress and jacket and a splendid white hat. Everything went well except for the strange arrival and departure of a woman in very elegant pale blue silk who spoke not a word to anyone.

'Who do you think that was?' Matt asked Sam.

Old Sam, buttoned up in his best suit of twenty years vintage, shook his head. 'I s'pose it must have been Christine's mother,' he said.

'But she didn't say a word! And now she's gone – without even drinking a toast to the happy pair.'

Sam sighed. 'That's an unhappy family,' he said. 'I gather from what Chrissie's let fall that her parents go their separate ways. I wonder if Joe is ever going to get to meet them?'

'You've met Mr Sharp, though, Grandad.'

'Oh aye. Came to the farm trying to throw his weight around. I dunno,' Sam said, looking perplexed. 'What do they hope to gain by pretending Chrissie and Joe haven't got wed?'

Matt had no idea. He had no time for further talk, however, for he had to carry out his role as best man. He'd looked it up in a book at Hotten Library and knew he had to make a speech and read out the telegrams of congratulations. One telegram came from Jack, and one from Annie's cousin Beryl Crossthwaite, but none from the Sharps.

His speech was brief. He thanked everyone who had to be thanked, managed a little joke about the Edwardian motif of the wedding as against Joe's modern view of farming, threatened to summon him back from his honeymoon if the tractor broke down again, and ended by saying that though they were going to live at Hawthorn, he knew there would be no thorns along the path of their married life.

'You did well, Matt,' Annie approved afterwards as the guests grouped themselves to chat once the happy couple had left for places unknown.

'I just said as little as I could,' Matt said. 'But mind you, I'd forgotten the father of the bride wouldn't be there to fill up the gaps. Rotten, that was – Henry did well tip-toeing through the minefields when he made his speech in place of Mr Sharp.'

Annie seemed to be watching the people helping themselves to refreshments. She said, without emphasis, 'There's a lot about today that's been strange, Matt. And a bit sad.'

'But Christine seemed to be on top of it, all the same.'

'Oh, aye. Being a bride sort of carries you along. Yet it must be a funny start to a marriage, being given away by someone other than your own father.'

'Henry was saying to me that of course the father of the bride is supposed to pay for a lot of the expenses, Ma. You haven't said how you're managing about the cost?'

'Well, Christine told Joe she had money put by.'

'That doesn't surprise me. The day I brought my things out of Hawthorn, I saw some of the stuff she's bought for the house. Expensive, it looked.'

'Her wedding dress—' Annie broke off.

'What about her wedding dress?'

'Nay, it's none of our business.'

'But what about it, Ma? Finish what you were going to say.'

'You know she bought it in Harrogate one day when Celia Winterton, Dry's fiancée, went with her? It came from a boutique. I looked in the window one afternoon when I was there with the Mother's Union outing – and the prices, Matt!'

'Well, you say she has money by her,' Matt reminded her.

'Yes, but . . .' Annie shook herself as if to rid herself of worrying thoughts. 'Well, Henry says you've got to look at it from the point of view of a girl who's got a dress allowance that would keep us in groceries for a couple of years. So I'm not going to think about it any more. Come on, Matt, let's go and have another glass of champagne before everybody else drinks it!'

Amused at her attitude – so unusual in Annie Sugden, who generally contented herself with half a glass of sherry at any celebration – Matt went with her. But by and by he slipped away from the crowd and went to stand under the old pear tree near the gate. The pears were turning rosy in the approaching autumn weather; they gleamed among the leaves like little lanterns. He looked up at them, remembering that when he and Peggy were married Annie had strung real lanterns in the tree to light them on their way as they left for their honeymoon.

He could see Alison at the buffet table, talking to the squire, Mr Verney. She looked relaxed and happy. It seemed it didn't bother her that if things had gone differently, she could have been looking forward to a wedding reception of her own. Or was he unjust to think she was insensitive? After all, no one looking at himself would think he was regretting the loss of his own happiness.

He frowned to himself. He must get out of this habit of going over his disappointment again and again. He wasn't the first man who'd hoped to marry a girl and found he wasn't wanted.

It was only that . . . well, he'd been so *sure* . . . He would have wagered everything he possessed on the certainty that Alison cared for him.

Alison, chatting to Mr Verney, glanced over her shoulder towards the boundary wall of the garden and the lane. There was someone standing in the shade of the pear tree. Somehow, without having to look again, she knew it was Matt.

Was I wrong to send him away? she asked herself. If I had been willing to compromise a little, if I'd played down my own actions – it might have worked out all right. We could have been looking forward today to our own wedding. Is that what he's thinking about as he stands there alone under the pear tree?

But no – he was probably thinking about Peggy. Poor Matt – at every turn he must find reminders of her. And the twins; although he adored them, each time he saw them he must remember that they had no mother, that he had to let his aunt take over their upbringing. Alison could have had the fun and the responsibility of looking after them if she had been less outspoken. Yet that had been one of the chief reasons for her frankness: it was unfair to saddle the twins with a stepmother who had a prison record.

When Verney was called away to speak to someone else, Alison had an impulse to go to Matt. But she checked herself. No, she mustn't do that. She mustn't weaken.

So she left Emmerdale after the reception having said no more than polite nothings to Matt. It seemed best.

The normal round was resumed on Monday. Matt had a long day ahead of him for he was helping a neighbour get in his barley. The dale worked its farms in this way at harvest time – men lent a hand to each other and expected the same in response. When he got home late that night, he thought Annie seemed a bit preoccupied but was too tired to speak to her about it. He ate his meal and fell into bed.

Next day was a repetition of Monday. The only difference was that Henry Wilks appeared at Littlewell to help with the harvesting, and as they sat together in the shade of a hedge at break time, drinking gallons of home-made lemonade to slake their thirst, Henry touched Matt's arm.

'Been up to Hawthorn recently?' he inquired.

'Me? No, why should I? I took my things out and put them in t'attic at Emmerdale.'

'I was up there yesterday. A delivery van had just left two antique elbow-chairs.'

'Oh aye?'

'I tell you, Matt, Joe's going to work all the hours God sends to make enough money.'

'For what?'

'To keep Christine in the style she's accustomed to.'

Matt took another draught of lemonade. 'Nay, Henry – she's a sensible girl. She's seen the way Joe lives at Emmerdale. She can't be expecting anything fancy.'

'Well, if she thinks Joe's going to come in from the fields and sit on those chairs, she's out of her mind. A bit of mud on his jacket and the upholstery will be ruined. To say nothing of his boots kicking the wood on the claw feet.'

'But she's thought of all that, I bet. She'll make loose covers or summat—'

'Matt, chairs like that don't get hidden behind loose covers. They're collectors' pieces. And those rugs on the floor are Persian, if I'm any judge.'

'Persian? Oh, come on, Henry—'

'I mean it. I'm worried, Matt. Something seems to have taken over in Christine since she got engaged to Joe.'

'But every woman likes to get a nice home together—'

'Of course. But a home that can't be lived in? Because Joe can never live the way he's used to, not in that house. She's turning it into a show place.'

'What, Hawthorn? But it's just a farm cottage—'

'No, it was a farmer's house, once. And it dates back to about 1800, the main part. She's furnishing it with pieces that belong to that era, and if I'm any judge the things she's put in already are worth best part of a thousand pounds.'

'A thousand?' Matt gasped. 'You're joking!'

'I'm not, you know. Those two chairs that were delivered yesterday are worth about five hundred pounds the pair. Add the cost of the rugs, and the dining-table – though I think *that's* a reproduction . . .'

There was a little silence.

'A thousand?' Matt said at last. And then, with what was for him unexpected irony, 'No wonder she didn't want Peg's uncut moquette!'

When work resumed part of his mind stayed with the words that Henry had spoken. For the first time Matt began to feel that he wasn't alone in having sensed something wrong in Christine. When she had shown herself determined to have Hawthorn, he'd been dismayed, but convinced himself it was only because the place was so special to him. Now Henry was saying that Christine had furnished the house after her own fashion, without regard to Joe's real comfort. And Annie had been voicing alarm over money matters when she spoke of the cost of the wedding dress.

Matt turned the combine harvester at the end of the field and went to the next swathe. He was thinking about Joe. Joe had seemed very distressed over the business of moving out Matt's belongings. Did Joe, too, sense that there was something steely in Christine's determination to have things the way she wanted? Certainly it was true that Matt had never thought Joe would fall for a girl who more or less forced her own view of life on him, a girl who at moments could be strangely blind to other people's feelings.

But then ... that was all to do with the wedding. Women in the throes of wedding preparations were like that – taken up with their own notions, almost obsessed that everything should be perfect.

When Christine and Joe came back, she would settle down with him to be a farmer's wife. She had to. That was her future. It was no use hoping to be the Lady of the Manor at Hawthorn – there was work to be done, and no one but Joe to do it. The way for Christine to be a good wife was to help Joe, not worry about the look of the house.

And as to the money side ... Well, that must all be an exaggeration. People ran away with wrong ideas so easily.

But not Henry Wilks, Matt thought uneasily. There was almost no one less likely to be run away with than hard-headed Henry Wilks.

Well, it would all come right once the bride and groom got back. Matt comforted himself with this thought and got on with his work.

Joe had managed to confine the honeymoon to a week in London despite schemes that had ranged over some of the more glamorous stretches of the Mediterranean. He knew very well that he was needed at home. You couldn't exactly say he regretted his honeymoon, because it had all been terrific – yet he'd had Emmerdale at the back of his mind all the while. He dared not let Christine see how glad he was to be going back when the Saturday came.

They were to take a train that got them in to Leeds at 4.12 p.m. Trouble began almost at once. Matt went to meet them with the Landrover, primed with instructions from Annie not to dilly-dally on the way back as she had a celebration tea planned. It was to be a big event – Old Sam had actually deigned to pick a bunch of sweet peas from his garden to grace the table.

But, as they approached Beckindale, it became clear to Matt that Christine expected to go to Hawthorn.

'Nay,' he murmured, 'I think you're expected at t'farm—'

'What? Nonsense!' she cried, giving him a playful slap on the arm. 'Joe and I want to go to our own home – don't we, Joe?'

'Well . . . yes . . . reckon that'd be best, Matt.'

'Are you sure, Joe? I think Ma . . .'

'There's all our luggage, anyhow,' Christine went on. 'We'd want to leave it there first in any case.'

Matt tried to catch Joe's eye, but Christine was pointing out the difference in the fields now that harvesting was well under way. It seemed there was no help for it. They were going to Hawthorn.

Matt tactfully busied himself with the luggage in the Landrover after they drew up. It gave Joe the opportunity to carry Christine over the threshold. He could hear from the laughter and cries of mock alarm that this was going on.

When he brought in their cases, Christine was standing in the middle of the living-room surveying the contents, a little frown on her face. 'I see the armchairs arrived,' she said over her shoulder to Matt.

'Eh? Oh, aye, Monday after you'd gone.'

'Who put them there?' she asked.

'How do you mean?'

'Someone's moved the table and put the chairs here, where it was standing.'

Matt stared at her. 'Well, *I* don't know,' he said. 'I heard the van came when we were all in t'fields – reckon the delivery men did it.'

'Oh yes.' Her face cleared. 'It's only that I wouldn't want anyone . . . altering . . .'

'I'm sure nobody would,' Joe said, studying the chairs. 'They look nice, don't they!'

'Not where they are, though. The table should be here.'

'Look, Christine,' he said, 'aren't you going to offer Matt a drink or anything?'

'Oh, goodness! Yes, of course! What must you think of me, Matt! After you were so kind, coming to the station and everything. Now would you like a glass of sherry, or a beer, or what?'

'Nay, I'd best get back to t'farm. Annie's expecting me.'

'Of course.'

'Er . . . Joe, you'll be coming along soon, eh?'

'You bet! I want to know whose crops've been got in so far—'

'But not before we've moved this table, Joe,' Christine put in.

'Shall I stop and give you a hand?' offered Matt.

'Nay, you get on. I'll only be a minute.'

'I think Annie's got a meal laid on,' Matt explained, trying not to sound insistent.

'Aye, I understand. See you in a minute.'

Matt drove on to Emmerdale. At the sound of the Landrover's engine, the door of the kitchen flew open, and Sam came rushing out. Matt had never seen him move so fast since his dog, Bess, had dragged him after a rabbit.

The old man drew back when Matt got out of the vehicle.

'Where's t'lad, then?' he asked. And then, alarmed, 'Nowt wrong?'

'Nay, they've gone to Hawthorn first.'

'Gone to Hawthorn? But didn't you tell 'em that Annie had baked gingerbread cake for 'em?'

'I didn't get the chance, Grandad. They were . . . well, you know, taken up with their own affairs. It's only natural.'

Annie appeared at the house door. 'Did they miss the train, Matt?'

'No, they were on it all right. But they've gone home—'

'Home?' she said, in surprise. And then, understanding, 'Oh, to Hawthorn.'

'That's right. He carried her ower t'threshold . . .' Matt smiled. 'They'll be along soon, Annie.'

But they were not. An hour went by, two hours. Old Sam became stridently hungry. 'I'm so empty, you could drive tractor through my innards,' he complained.

'All right, then, Dad, we'll have us teas.'

'But we can't start wi'out *them*,' he said. 'It'll spoil t'look of things if you cut into the pie!'

'All right then, we'll wait.'

'But I'm hungry.'

'Then I'll cut you a bit of bread and cheese to be going on.'

'But that'll spoil my appetite for proper tea.'

'What d'you want, then, Dad?' she asked in a tone of calm reason. 'To have a full stomach or a good cause of complaint? Just tell me.'

'I want my tea at teatime,' he said. 'It's past teatime by now.'

'I know what time it is, Dad.'

'But them youngsters don't, it seems.'

'We were unreasonable,' she said. 'We should have realized they'd want to spend an hour or two in their own home before they came to see us.'

'To see us?' Sam said, in a voice that suddenly trembled, making him seem for once an old man. 'But this is his home – you don't come to see folks in your own home.'

'But his home's Hawthorn now,' his daughter reminded him. 'We mustn't forget that.'

They arrived at last. The time was almost seven o'clock. Matt was sorry now that he'd admitted he'd said a meal was waiting for them. For Joe knew full well that tea at Emmerdale meant five-thirty – so they were now an hour and a half late.

Strange to say, the one who was most angry was Sam. It had nothing to do with the fact that he was hungry. As the minutes ticked by he became more and more aware of the affront to his daughter, who had cooked all this lovely food for a homecoming party which the youngsters didn't even have the grace to attend.

'So here you are at last,' he said to Joe as they came in. 'Thought you couldn't find the way here.'

'Sorry, Grandad. There were a couple of things Christine wanted to attend to.'

'Yes, do you know,' Christine exclaimed, 'that those men who delivered our armchairs had had the cheek to shunt our table over to make room for them?'

'I did that,' Annie said.

'What?'

'I moved the table and put the chairs where they are now. I thought it was where you'd want them.'

'Oh – did you? Well, I–'

'You got it all wrong, Ma,' Joe laughed. 'We've spent the last couple of hours pushing furniture around trying to get the . . . the what, Christine?'

'The balance right. There's a natural balance in the arrangement of a room, you see.'

'Happen,' Annie said. She had always put furniture where it was most needed: balance or otherwise never came into it. 'I'll mash tea, shall I?'

Over the meal, conversation was strange. From time to time moments of strain arose, in a way that Matt had never experienced before at Emmerdale. Christine spoke of London in terms of shops and restaurants; Joe remembered chiefly the horses of the Lifeguards, the lorries laden with farm produce trundling into Covent Garden. When Sam inquired after the flowers in the parks, Christine couldn't recall what they had been: 'The usual stiff herbaceous borders of dahlias and things, I suppose.'

'Not dahlias,' Sam protested. 'Couldn't be dahlias yet – it's too early.'

'I really don't remember,' she said, and turned to Annie to describe a fashion-in-fur show she had been to at Harrods.

'I think there were dahlias, Grandad,' Joe volunteered. 'Things are earlier down there than they are up here. You should have seen the fruit in the shops – funny things with names like grenadine and passion fruit.'

'Seen 'em at the Royal Yorkshire,' Sam said. 'Passion fruit. They had a special show one year. Full of pips, stained your fingers red.'

'No, that's a pomegranate, Grandad.' Joe turned to Matt. 'Got your ewes sorted out for the show, then?'

'Aye, I reckon I've picked 'em.'

'What d'you think then. Going to win?'

'Don't see why not.'

'Big competition there, lad,' Sam said. 'Best show in t'north, is that.'

'He knows that, Grandad. He's only whistling to keep his courage up.'

'Nowt o't'sort,' Matt said, deadpan. 'Reckon I'm going to walk off with Best in Show.'

'What're you exhibiting, then? Hedgehogs?'

'Let me tell you, Joe Sugden, them ewes will take some beating.'

'All this modesty will get you nowhere,' Joe said. 'Reckon you really have any chance, though?'

'We-ell . . . I think they're a good bunch. You remember that lamb your Ma raised two year agone—'

'Joe,' Christine put in, 'I'm talking to you.'

'What? What – oh, did you speak, Chris?'

'I'm asking you what was the name of that place we went to on the river where they had paintings on the ceiling. You remember – near the museum.'

'Er ... Greenwich, I think. The Queen's House, was it called?'

'That's it! You see, Mrs Sugden, the paintings gave an impression of space – *trompe l'oeil*, it's called, I think.'

'Oh yes?' Annie said. A little silence fell round the table. Joe, cut off in the middle of what he'd been discussing with Matt, had lost the thread. His grandfather was staring at Christine in amazement. Interrupting the men folk when they were talking about the Royal Yorkshire—! What were things coming to?

Christine, quite unaware that everything else had ceased, went on with her description of how to use the technique of *trompe l'oeil* to make an ordinary living-room look bigger.

When the meal was over the newlyweds took their leave. 'You must all come to dinner with me tomorrow,' Christine said. 'The first time I'll have had guests.'

'Nay,' said Sam, 'you don't want to have us there in the middle of the day – we're all hard at work on harvesting, we'll be all mucky and dusty.'

'But I didn't mean midday, Grandad. I was talking about the evening.'

'But you said dinner.'

'I meant evening dinner. You will come, won't you?'

Melted by her smile and her special invitation to him, he smiled back and said he'd be delighted.

He had no idea what a mistake he was making. It meant he would have to wait until seven-thirty to eat, and wear his stiff best suit into the bargain.

CHAPTER NINE

For Joe the next day began badly and ended worse.

He was up at the usual hour to go to Emmerdale for the milking. Christine made as if to get up, but he kissed her on the nose and told her to stay where she was. Downstairs in the kitchen, he made instant coffee because he couldn't find the tea, and was out of the house by five-thirty.

Matt was already in the milking parlour. He nodded a welcome. 'Funny to see you coming in from outside,' he said. 'Couldn't think where you were this morning, in t'kitchen.'

'Well, we'll all get used to it. You're glad to have me back, I take it.'

'Couldn't have lived another minute without you. Besides, grandad's so bad-tempered first thing in t'morning.'

'Did Ma help you sometimes?'

'Aye, but that's not fair on her. She's enough to do.'

'That's right. No need from now on, though. Christine'll be here for evening milking as usual.'

'Isn't that a bit much for her, though?' Matt observed. 'I mean, she's got you to look after now. And a dinner party 's'evening.'

'Oh, that makes no odds. She's got it all planned out. Been thinking it out for days.'

'Go on,' said Matt.

'Yes, menu all planned. She's determined to be a super housewife.'

'I still think it's a lot for the lass, coming trudging over here to work, and then back to get your meals and that.'

'What's the alternative?' Joe responded. 'We can only manage financially if Chris has a job – and if she's working for Emmerdale Farm she's got to pull her weight.'

'Aye, I suppose so.' Matt considered. 'Couldn't you manage on your own wages? It's mainly food and heating, that's all, isn't it?'

'But you've got to reckon on the bills that will come in,' Joe said.

'Bills?'

'For the wedding reception, and furniture Chrissie's bought, and stuff like that. We've got to pay for all that by and by.'

'I see. A few months might do it, though?'

'I don't know,' Joe said, with a frown. 'I've never quite reckoned up what the bills are going to be. Chris says they'll send an account.'

They worked on in silence for the rest of the stint. At eight-thirty, Annie came out to say that breakfast was on the table.

'You staying, Joe?'

'No, Chris'll be expecting me,' he said, and with a cheery wave started off on the shortcut across the fields to Hawthorn.

When he came indoors he was greeted with a faint shriek of protest from his wife. 'Don't come in in those boots!' she cried. 'Go round the kitchen door.'

He backed out and did as he was bid. In the kitchen he found everything spick and span, a bowl of brilliant marigolds arranged on the table, but no breakfast.

'Chris!' he called.

'Just a minute!'

'Chris, are we having breakfast in there?'

She appeared at the kitchen door, in jeans and a loose smock, with a spray can of polish in one hand and a duster in the other.

'Nobody's going in there until we have the dinner party,' she told him in smiling menace. 'I've got it almost perfect.'

'So what are we having for breakfast?' he inquired. 'Fried duster and polish sauce?'

'Oh . . . breakfast . . . is it breakfast time already?'

'It's half past eight, Chris.'

'Didn't you think of staying at Emmerdale?'

'Ma asked me, but I said I'd rather come home.' He pointed at the marigolds, and said, 'I can't eat those, Chrissie.'

'No – of course not, I'm sorry. I've been so busy I lost track of time. What'll you have?'

'Bacon and egg's quickest.'

'Right. Just a minute while I finish polishing the—'

'I'll do it, shall I?' he offered. He turned towards the fridge.

'Don't you dare! You had coffee before you went out, didn't you?'

'Well . . . yes.'

'You left your dirty cup and saucer on the table, and forgot to put the lid back on the coffee jar.'

'Oh, did I? I'm sorry. Only I couldn't find the tea caddy.'

'We haven't got a caddy,' she said. 'Don't you remember? Mrs Dawkins gave us a tea-dispenser.' She touched a container screwed to the wall near the cooker.

'Is that what it is?' cried Joe. 'I never understood it.' He went to it and thumbed the tab on the top. A measure of tea came out at the bottom and fell straight on the floor.'

'Oh, Joe!' cried Christine. 'Now look what you've done! What a mess!'

'It's only tea,' he protested.

'Sit down. Don't move. I'll be back in a minute to make your breakfast.'

He did as he was bid. She finished the polishing, but even then he had to wait while she brushed up the spilled tea with a dustpan and brush.

While she cooked the bacon he told her the news from the farm. 'Matt says he's glad to have me back,' he said. 'Grandad's too old to be turned out of bed at dawn. It really needs a regular team like us.'

'Oh . . . well, of course, I'll be back as usual tomorrow, Joe. But for today, I think I'd rather stay at home. I've a lot to do.'

'Nothing too important, really,' he said. 'Only the dinner party.'

'*Only* the dinner party? I want everything to be perfect.'

'Yes, of course. But don't knock yourself out over it, Christine.'

She served his food, and sat down opposite with a slice of toast and a cup of tea. 'You know,' she mused, 'it would be a good idea to build an outhouse on to the outside of this door.'

'A what?'

'An outhouse. A sort of vestibule. So's you could leave your work-clothes there before you come into the kitchen.'

Joe swallowed a large mouthful of bacon. 'We don't have an outhouse at Emmerdale.'

'No . . . Well, it would be a good idea there, too. Save your mother a lot of work cleaning floors.'

'Ma doesn't complain.'

'She comes of a generation that took work as part of the scheme of things. These days we can see it's better to plan to ease the work-load.'

'Now you sound like the girl from the Low Cost Production department!'

'But it's true, Joe. Labour-saving is sense. That's why I think our first investment ought to be a washing machine.'

'A washing machine?' Joe was aghast.

'Don't sound so amazed. Every home should have one.'

'But Peg always used to bring her wash down to Emmerdale and put it in with Ma's.'

'That's not so convenient for me, though, is it? I mean, I'm going to be working – Peggy was at home with the twins while she lived here.'

'But I'd have thought, since you were coming across to Emmerdale anyway, it would make more sense to bring the washing—'

'What, hump it all across the field?'

'I'll carry it for you.'

'Except when you forget, or are going somewhere else. No, Joe we really must have one of our own.'

'But I don't see why it should be so high on the list of priorities. I thought—'

'You don't begrudge me a washing machine, do you, Joe?'

'Of course not. By and by you can have one, and a freezer if you want one—'

'I'd rather have the washing machine as a priority. And we must get that floor in the living-room sanded and polished—'

'Yes, there's a firm I've heard of—'

'And once it's done, mind, Joe, no coming in through the front door with those boots on. We don't want it scratched.'

'You will actually let me in the house?' he asked, only half joking.

'It's just that I want to keep the place looking nice, Joe. There's no pleasure in a home that's looking uncared for.'

'But it isn't exactly comfortable to live in a show-house, Christine.'

'That's the wrong attitude,' she scolded. 'You want to take a pride in where we live and take little precautions to keep it nice.'

'If you mean being stopped on the doorstep and made to undress – that'll be no fun in the winter.' He hoped by joking about it to make her see the absurdity.

'By that time we'll have the outhouse built,' she said.

Joe got up and went to the door.

'Aren't you going to eat up your bacon?' she said.

'I've got to get back. I were late before you started cooking, and now I've overstayed breakfast time by quarter of an hour.'

'Oh, Joe, as if it matters on your first day back!'

He opened the kitchen door and went out. He paused and turned. 'I'll be back for dinner – I mean midday dinner – at twelve-thirty. You'd better put a pair of slippers here if you want me to change before I step inside the house.'

But to his horror, she did just that.

He marched in, disregarding them. A meal of cold ham and pickle and cheese was on a plate covered by another plate. Christine had left a note: 'Gone to Hotten to buy ingredients for tonight.'

In silence he ate the food. He then set about making a pot of tea, but the tea dispenser defeated him – one measure went on the outside of the pot and the other stuck in the outlet of the dispenser. He made coffee again, carefully screwing the lid on the jar with so much assiduity that he cracked the plastic and the thing wouldn't close.

'Oh, damn it all,' he growled, and banged it down on the work surface. The top flew off in two pieces and coffee granules sprayed all over everything.

He swept it all up. He drank his coffee. He put his dirty plate in the sink and ran the tap on it. He went back to work. He was thoroughly fed up.

During the afternoon Henry paid a visit to the farm. 'Hello, young feller-me-lad,' he said cheerfully. 'Married life agreeing with you?'

'Like a charm,' Joe said, in a tone whose irony escaped Henry.

'Met your missus in Beckindale on her way to Hotten. She's invited me to this "do" tonight.'

'That's good,' Joe said. He had no idea whether it was or not.

'Sounds like the food will be marvellous. We're having grouse, I hear – *aux truffes*.'

'Whatever that means.'

'Oh, you'll enjoy it. *Haute cuisine*, that is.'

'I thought it were game-bird.'

Henry eyed him. He wasn't sure whether his leg was being pulled. 'Eeh, it's nice to have you back,' he said. 'In good time for the Yorkshire. I'm going to be there to cheer for Matt.'

'That's what Grandad says.'

'Oh, aye, we must all go.'

'We can't all go, Henry. Somebody's got to be here to do milking.'

'Oh aye . . .' Henry was from time to time brought up short by reminders like this. Try as he would, he couldn't become the complete farmer; he still felt his time was his own.

'I'll sort it out,' Joe said. And later, in the barn, he remarked to Matt, 'Seems like a big cheer-party from Emmerdale will be going to t'Show.'

'Grandad certainly intends to do his bit,' Matt agreed.

'Ma wants to go too.'

'Ye-es.' Matt understood at once that they were talking about milking. 'We could get someone in, just the once—'

'Nay, most of Beckindale will be at t'Show. Listen, I reckon it's our turn to stay at home while the rest of you go out gadding. Chrissie and I will see to milking.'

'But Chrissie would want to go—'

'I don't think she's bothered. She hasn't mentioned it at all.'

'We'll ask her when she comes for evening milking.'

Joe cleared his throat. 'Well . . . er . . . in fact she won't be here.'

'Eh?'

'Well, this dinner party, y'know . . . she's all of a fret. She's gone to Hotten this afternoon to get stuff, and I think she'll be pottering about t'kitchen from now till dinner-time. See here, Matt, that's one more reason why us two should stay home while you all go to t'Show. We've gadded about while you've held the fort. It's our turn to let you do a bit of gadding.'

'Well . . . yes . . . but this evening, Joe . . .'

'Will you do it with me? Don't want to ask Grandad – you

know how he is. And Ma's pressing his suit and a dress for this evening ... All this fuss,' Joe sighed. 'I know you were supposed to be off at four, but—'

'It's all right,' Matt said. 'I were only going to talk to Geoff Brightstaff about sending a pot plant to Auntie Beattie and Uncle Bert. It's their anniversary tomorrow. Won't take a minute.'

'Thanks, Matt. I appreciate it.'

Matt went across the fields and by the wood path to see the nurseryman. He came out on the edge of the oak spinney to see two figures in the distance, higher up the slope, standing turned towards each other in deep conversation.

Alison and Henry.

His heart sank. He knew that Henry had been made a confidant of Alison's long before his own close relationship with her. He had always feared Henry as a rival much more likely to win her. And now, when a coolness had developed between himself and Alison, it was only natural that Henry should step in.

If he could have heard their talk, he would have been reassured on at least one score.

'I beg you to think carefully,' Henry was saying. 'It's not often in my life I've pleaded with anyone, but I'm doing it now.'

'I have thought, Henry.'

'Then think again. You have a good life here – friends who really care for you, a job you enjoy ...'

'I know that. It doesn't seem to compensate ...'

'For what?' He took her hand in both of his and pressed it. 'Compensate for what? The things in the past?'

'No, that's not it. That's a separate thing.'

'Then ... is it something to do with Matt?'

She turned away and began to walk again, but he retained his hold of her hand, so that from the distance it appeared as if they were strolling along linked in close friendship.

'I don't want to talk about it,' she said.

'But that's hardly fair, Alison. You tell me you're leaving Beckindale to start up a new venture with Louise in Jersey, but you don't say why.'

'I think it would be profitable. And challenging.'

'Profitable? You mean in money terms? You've never been one to put money first. And as for challenge – surely there's challenge enough here?'

She made no reply.

'It's something to do with Matt,' he insisted. 'I thought for a while there, that you and he . . . But then it stopped dead.'

'Please let's change the subject—'

'What happened? Did you feel obliged to tell him?'

'Henry, I only told you I was going because we have to settle what to do about the shop—'

'You told Matt – that's it, isn't it?' Henry stopped. 'It couldn't have made any difference to him?' he exclaimed.

'Listen, Henry. Matt isn't a free agent in the same way as you. He's got two little ones to think of—'

'Dammit, Matt isn't the sort to count up past mistakes against you in that way! I can't believe it.' Despite sharp twinges of jealousy that Henry had felt over Matt during the summer now coming to its close, he had never for one moment doubted that Matt deserved Alison.

'I'd like you to buy back your share of the shop at the price you sold it to me,' Alison said.

'It's worth a lot more now,' he replied automatically, his businessman's mind taking over.

'I don't care. I just want you to buy it back – I don't want to make a profit.'

'But you're entitled to benefit from your own labours—'

'I just want to settle it all as quickly as possible. Please, Henry.'

He sighed. 'Say what you want and it shall be done.'

'On a business footing.'

'Damn it, woman, how can I deal with you on a business footing? I'm in love with you!'

'We can have the stock valued if you feel that's necessary—'

Henry seized her by the upper arms, quite fiercely. 'Why don't you marry me and let me look after you?' he demanded. 'It'd save a lot of trouble and worry!'

She leaned back to indicate that she wanted him to release his grasp. 'If I could, or wanted to, Henry, I wouldn't. How would Matt feel?'

And the converse of that, he realized later as he was dressing for dinner, was – how could she marry Matt without hurting himself?

She was caught in a perfect trap. Unwittingly, he and Matt had made it almost impossible for Alison to remain in Beckindale.

At the farm, the family were getting ready to go out to dinner. Annie, well aware that her father would start to complain about hunger long before it was time to eat, had given him a hearty snack at four-thirty. But now at about twenty-past-seven he was sitting in the kitchen in his good suit with his feet together and his hands clasped on his stick, ready to leap up and go. His stomach told him it was long past tea-time.

'Sit back, Dad,' Annie recommended. 'We won't be leaving for ten minutes or so.'

'But that'll mean we'll be late. She asked us to be there at seven-thirty.'

'But she didn't expect us to turn up till about a quarter-to-eight.'

'Don't be daft,' Sam said. 'If she said seven-thirty, she meant seven-thirty.'

'It's not the done thing to arrive absolutely on time.'

'Yes it is. I remember it in my copybook when I were at school. "Punctuality is the politeness of Princes." '

'Well, that were fifty year agone. The thing now is to turn up a bit after you were told. Some people don't thank you for being on time.'

'I don't understand that,' Sam said. 'Folks should say what they mean . . .'

'You'd better sit back and relax, Grandad,' Matt advised. 'Henry promised to collect us, to save us turning up in t'Landrover. So we can't go until he comes.' Matt was polishing his shoes prior to putting them on. He too was in his good suit.

Annie was in the two-piece she had worn for the wedding. She felt strangely perturbed. She couldn't understand herself – she was only going for a meal with her daughter-in-law, so why all the anxiety? Why all the dressing up?

Yet it had been necessary. She had acknowledged that by spending the afternoon pressing all their clothes. Somehow the importance of the event had communicated itself to her. But important to whom?

Henry arrived, looking smart in a dark suit. To tell the truth, he had actually contemplated putting on his dinner jacket, but second thoughts had reminded him that neither Sam nor Matt would have one. Yet when they got to Hawthorn he too understood that this was a very important engagement. Christine looked a picture.

She was wearing a long dress of flowered crepe with a frill round the ankles, and her thick brown hair was done up on top of her head in a little knot. She approached with her hands out to greet them.

'Welcome to Hawthorn,' she exclaimed.

Had she forgotten that they had all been there many times before, when Peggy was the hostess?

Certainly the place looked different. You had to hand it to her, thought Henry. She had taste. The rich, well-hung curtains, the gleam on the antique furniture, the table spread with what looked like Royal Worcester and what was certainly silver . . .

They had a pre-dinner drink. Old Sam looked as if he might protest at this but when he tried the sherry he changed his mind. All the same, he couldn't help remarking, 'Dinner won't be long, I s'pose?'

'The first course is all ready,' Christine told him, dropping a kiss on the top of his head as she passed to hand Henry his drink.

The first course was pâté. Old Sam, with the aid of his newly acquired glasses, had no difficulty identifying it. 'Potted meat!' he cried. 'Nothing I like better than a bit of potted meat.'

'This potted meat happens to be pâté, all the way from France,' Joe informed him with a grin. 'Have some toast.'

'Toast? What's toast for? We having baked beans too?'

'It's to eat the pâté with,' Joe persisted.

'I don't need toast, I've got lettuce and that.' And so saying, Sam picked up a knife and fork from among the array by his plate and ate his potted meat.

The main course was the grouse. Christine had spent hours getting it just right with all the trimmings – breadcrumbs, watercress, little snippets of bread with the truffles on, game chips.

The first hiatus arrived when it came to carving. Joe, as head of the house, was expected to handle this. He struggled with the birds, and succeeded in getting one right off the serving dish. 'Eh,' he said, 'I don't know as anybody's going to get any of this, I'm making such a hash of it.'

'Then give it to your Ma,' Sam said, watching it all with his mouth watering. 'She's a dab hand.'

Without consulting Christine, Joe rose and carried the serving dish to Annie. Annie, never imagining it could be wrong to help, carved the grouse and sent the dish round the table for the guests to help themselves.

'No vegetables?' Sam asked, looking at the grouse on his plate.

'Joe, will you hand them round?'

Joe leapt up and brought the vegetable dishes to his grandfather. Sam, accustomed to having potatoes and greens put on his plate by his daughter, looked at the serving dishes with surprise. 'My, we are posh tonight,' he said with a smile.

Henry happened to be looking at Christine at that moment. He saw her lips tighten.

The grouse was good, but the little fiddly bits bothered the contingent from Emmerdale. Only Henry knew what to do, how much of each item to take. Joe, at a nod from Christine, kept topping up the wine glasses. If Annie thought it strange that the man of the house had to keep interrupting his meal to serve the guests, she didn't let it show.

'The birds are done to a turn,' she said in compliment to Christine.

'Thank you. Will you have some more watercress, Matt?'

'Nay, I took too much t'first time,' he said. 'This stuff on the little bit of bread is all right – what is it, Chris?'

'Truffle.'

'Truffle? But that's stuff you put in chocolates, isn't it?'

'Nay, it's a fungus you find in France,' Henry said. 'They use it a lot.'

'Like mushrooms, you mean.'

'More expensive than mushrooms, I'm afraid,' Henry said. 'I've been at a country market in France when they brought in the truffles to sell, and I can tell you they cost a packet.'

'Now he tells me,' groaned Joe, laughing.

Christine said sharply, 'If you're going to prepare a classic recipe, it isn't worth economizing on the ingredients.'

'Nice, this is,' Sam remarked, chewing. 'I'n't very filling, though.'

He didn't find the sweet course very filling either. It proved to be pears in wine. The shallow dish was passed round; after counting heads, Sam helped himself to two pieces. Then he looked up again. 'No custard?' he asked.

'Now, Dad,' his daughter reproved.

'Don't you have custard with this? Oh well . . .' he picked up his spoon.

'We could give him some cream,' Joe suggested. 'I saw a tin in the larder.'

'Tinned cream with pears in wine?' Christine said, in a tone that told him he had committed a crime.

'These are really lovely,' Henry put in hastily. 'Local pears, are they?'

'Yes. And the wine's French Burgundy.'

Henry thought of the price of a bottle of French Burgundy, and ate in silence.

They rose from the table and transferred themselves to comfortable chairs for the coffee. Old Sam was about to protest at the size of the demi-tasse he was handed, but a glance from Annie quelled him. Cream appeared, but not from a tin. Sam put too much in his cup and some went over on to the floor. It made a little white puddle on the Persian rug.

'Oops, I've dropped some on your runner,' he said.

Christine, pouring, looked up. 'Runner?' she said.

'Your rug – sorry, lass.'

She saw the spot, and her hand shook. Coffee went over the side of the coffee tray on to her lap. She leapt up, crying out with the heat of the coffee as it soaked through, but more in distress at the stain on her dress – and the stain on the Persian rug.

'I'll fetch a cloth,' Joe said, hurrying to the kitchen. He was back in a moment, attempting to sponge the dress. She seized the cloth and instead began to mop up the cream on the rug.

'Nay, lass,' Annie said, 'you'll only spread it like that. There's butter fat in cream – you'll make a mark.'

Christine sat back on her heels.

'A drop of washing up liquid, that's what you need.'

'I'll get it—'

'Nay, Joe, I'll get it.' Annie went into the kitchen. When she got back with the container, Joe was trying to help Christine clean the rug.

'Leave me alone,' Christine told him, almost in tears. 'Pour the coffee for the others, for heavens' sake!'

Joe, startled, got up off his knees. Annie knelt in his place and rubbed gently at the mark. After a moment it began to look cleaner. 'There,' she said. 'Look at it again in the morning and if it isn't completely gone, have another go with just a drop of liquid on a warm cloth. That'll do it.'

Christine got up. The place where she had spilt the coffee on herself was now a dark, clinging stain on her skirt. 'I'd better go and change,' she said in a tone of utter despair, quite out of keeping with the situation.

When she had gone, an awkward silence fell.

'I'm sorry,' Sam said, very subdued. 'That were my fault. I should have been more careful. I didn't know she set such a value on the runner.'

'It's a Persian carpet, Sam,' Henry explained.

'Oh.'

Another silence. 'A spot of anything?' Joe inquired, too bright. 'Whisky, brandy?'

'I wouldn't mind a whisky,' Henry said. He felt a bit guilty, drinking their spirits at the price they were – for owning half-shares in a pub made Henry very conscious of the cost. Yet he felt he was being helpful in accepting the offer.

Matt, too, caught on, and said he would have a small brandy. They sat in awkward constraint with their glasses in their hands.

'Well, here's to a happy future at Hawthorn,' Henry said at last.

Everybody looked at everybody else. If there were many evenings like this one, the future looked grim.

With determination, Henry began to talk about the only thing that he knew would interest everyone – the harvest which was now just going past its peak.

When Christine came back, in a different dress and with her lipstick freshened, she found them all deep in an argument about who would buy Mr Verney's land if it was true, as rumoured, that he was selling up. She sat by, saying nothing, feeling excluded because she had never met Verney.

The guests had arrived at a quarter-to-eight. By a quarter-past-ten they had all had enough. 'We must go,' Annie said, getting up. 'Milking at five-thirty as usual, I'm afraid.'

'Oh, but you don't all have to go . . .' She turned to Henry. 'You'll stay awhile, Henry?'

'Sorry, Christine, I'm their transport.'

'Oh . . . But you could come back after you've dropped them off. *You* don't have to be up for milking.'

'No, but I do,' Joe reminded her.

'But we've stayed up later than this many a time, Joe,' she said, her face small and white with disappointment as her dinner party dispersed in trickles of embarrassment.

'You've done enough, love,' Annie told her kindly. 'You've had a long day. It's time we went.' She kissed her gently on the cheek. 'Goodnight, Christine, see you tomorrow. Thanks for a lovely time.'

They all murmured that they had enjoyed themselves tremendously. Henry added a commendation of the food. The young couple went out to wave them off in Henry's car.

When they came back in, Christine began to collect up coffee cups and wine glasses.

'Leave that, love,' Joe begged. 'We'll do it tomorrow.'

'Tomorrow? I don't want to come down to this wreckage.'

'I'll do it before you're up—'

'No, that wouldn't be fair. I'll do it now.'

Seeing she was determined, he helped her gather up the debris and dried the dishes as she washed. She worked in silence. And in the silence it became more difficult to think of what to say to her.

When the last plate had been stacked away and the last glass polished, they went up to bed. Joe watched her unpin her hair, with jerky little movements.

'Why does it matter so much, Christine?' he asked.

She paused. 'I wanted it all to be perfect.'

'But . . . don't you think you tried too hard?'

'Of course I *tried*. I planned it all to the last detail – and it went wrong from the beginning.'

'I always said that food was too fancy for the likes of Grandad—'

'Oh yes, go on, tell me "I told you so"!'

'Nay, love ... I didn't mean that. But they'd have been happy with cold meat and a warm welcome.'

'You mean that I wasn't welcoming to them? They were the very first guests I invited!'

'But you were trying to impress them, not please them—'

'You don't understand!' she burst out. 'It should have been a lovely evening – why didn't it go properly?'

'You were all keyed up. Chrissie, you're still keyed up. You're right, I don't understand it. You made it seem like the first night of some play ...'

In his mind he heard the echo of the words her father had spoken to him when they happened upon each other at Loudwick market. 'She gets fantasies and follows them. At the moment the fantasy is to be a farmer's wife ...'

Was this what was wrong? Was her fantasy of the perfect dinner party given by the young bride so important to her?

'Oh, love,' he said gently and went behind her at the dressing-table to put his arms around her.

She bent her head. He couldn't see her reflection in the mirror. After a moment she said in a flat voice, 'Your mother was right. It's been a long day.'

'I know, lass. Come on, let's get to bed.'

When he came out of the bathroom she was already under the covers, eyes closed, one arm thrown over the lower half of her face. He leaned over to kiss her before he got in beside her. He thought she would move her arm for his kiss, but she did not. He touched her cheek with his lips, and lay down.

He was tired. He fell asleep. But he woke while it was still dark, and he thought he heard her crying.

'Chrissie?' he muttered. 'You all right?'

No reply. Her breathing, when he leaned closer, seemed steady and even.

All the same, he was sure she had been crying, and that she was awake though she pretended to be asleep.

Baffled, he lay in the darkness wondering what had gone wrong that they could lay unspeaking after only nine days of married life.

CHAPTER TEN

Matt came in from milking next morning to find Old Sam waiting eagerly for him. 'A letter for you,' he said, nodding towards the dresser where mail was left after the postman brought it.

'Oh, aye?' said Matt, thinking it would be a thing from some government department about insurance stamps or the like.

'Foreign, it is,' Sam said. Now he could see everything, thanks to his new spectacles, little escaped his eagle eye.

'Foreign?' Matt echoed, and went to fetch it.

True enough, it had a stamp unlike any that Matt had seen before, and a postmark, which, though smudged, seemed to be in a foreign tongue.

He studied it for a while.

'Well?' demanded Sam. 'Who's it from?'

'Now, Dad, that's none of our business,' Annie said, bringing kidneys and fried mushrooms to the table. 'How much toast, Matt?'

'Two slices, please.' He put the letter in his pocket.

'Aren't you going to open it?' Sam asked, astounded.

'Haven't time. I've got to get back out to them ewes. They've got to be perfect for t'Show.'

The truth was that he was inflicting a tease on Sam. By and by he would tell the old man what was in the letter – but it would never do to spoil the joke by opening it at once.

After breakfast, up on Blea Head, he took it out again. Renewed examination of the stamp suggested to him that it was Irish, although he'd never to his recollection seen an Irish stamp before. He prised open the envelope.

Inside was a small sheet of paper, such as one might get from a pocket notebook. The message upon it, written in a strong firm hand, was brief.

'Dear Matt, As I was about to say when we were interrupted – marry the girl! Regards, Dry.'

A letter from Dry! It was the last thing Matt had ever expected. So he'd gone to Ireland? As far away from his fiancée as he could get, it seemed.

He re-read the message. A fine one to be giving another man advice about his love-life – Dry, who couldn't face up to his own emotional commitments.

Marry the girl ... He meant Alison, of course. They had been talking about Alison the night Celia Winterton walked into the Woolpack and Dry took his hasty departure.

Even if it was true that Dry couldn't handle his own affairs, that didn't mean he lacked shrewdness when he observed those of others. He had seen what Matt had sensed – that Alison cared for him.

Perhaps he had given up too easily after her rejection. For a time he'd shied away from having to examine what she said on that occasion, but now he sat thinking about it on the stone dyke on the ridge, he wondered if she had actually said she didn't love him, couldn't love him.

He must think about it. There might be a chance for them both, if he went back and asked again.

Henry came to the farm at lunchtime, as he often did, so as to share the delights of Annie's cooking. 'Not as fancy as last night, I'm afraid,' she said as she put a heaped plate of boiled gammon before him.

'Eeh, this is grand,' he said, almost rubbing his hands with appreciation. He ate for a moment, then said in a neutral tone, 'Interesting evening.'

Sam paused with a mouthful of spinach en route to his mouth. 'I never thought that runner would be so important,' he said, half apologetic and half complaining. 'Didn't look much to me.'

'You have to be a bit of an expert to see the value,' Henry said. 'Worth about sixty quid, I think, that one.'

'Never!'

'It's the truth.'

Sam ate his spinach. Then he said, anxious and not complaining, 'What's she want a thing like that for, in her living-room? I don't understand it.'

'Everybody has their own views on how to furnish their home, Dad,' Annie said. She met Henry's eyes and shook her head slightly to warn him not to pursue the topic.

'Joe eating at home, then?' Henry said, taking a sidestep.

'Aye, but he'll be back by two. Chrissie came to fetch him, says she'll be here this afternoon for the milking.'

'That's all right then,' Henry said, hoping it was true.

When the meal was over, Matt set out for a neighbour's farm where the barley was being brought in. 'Mind if I walk part of the way?' Henry said.

They set out together. For a time they talked about the farm and the forthcoming Yorkshire Show. Then Henry said, 'I wanted a word with you about Alison.'

Matt braced himself. After that view of them talking so earnestly yesterday, he felt sure Henry was going to say he had proposed to Alison and been accepted. Too late to get a letter of encouragement from Dry . . .

'She's leaving, did you know?'

'What? Oh aye – holiday. Training up Mrs Dawkins to take her place while she's away.'

'No,' Henry said in a heavy tone. 'She's talking about selling up and going for good.'

They walked on without further words for a moment.

'She hasn't mentioned it to you?' Henry said at length.

Matt shook his head. 'We haven't had much chance to talk . . . Harvest, you know, and that . . .'

'Mmmm . . . I think it's a bit of a sudden decision. And I think it's a mistake.'

'Do you? But if it's what she wants . . ?'

'I don't think she knows what she wants. And I certainly don't think she should rush into a big decision like that while she's . . . upset.'

'What makes you think she's upset, then?'

'Dunno. I thought you might have some idea about that.'

Matt made no response to that. Gimbel's Farm hove up on the slope, the place where he was going to help with the barley. 'Alison didn't speak to me about leaving,' Matt murmured.

'She had to confide in me because of the shop,' Henry said, answering the objection unstated in Matt's remark.

'Aye, that's true.'

'I don't know what might make her change her mind,' Henry went valiantly on. 'Anyway, thought I'd mention it to you.'

'Aye . . .'

'So long then, Matt.'

'So long, Henry.'

Matt waved a farewell as Henry continued on the road to the bridge and Beckindale, while he himself took the footpath to Gimbel's.

He understood very well what Henry had been saying to him. 'I tried to persuade Alison to stay but she wouldn't change her mind for my sake. So I withdraw, Matt – see if she'll change her mind for *you.*'

He certainly was going to have a try. It wouldn't be right to let her go without making a last attempt to let her know how much he loved and needed her.

Joe joined him at Gimbel's for the afternoon's work. To Matt's eye he looked downhearted. 'Anything wrong?' he asked.

'Nowt serious. Just that I've had a bit of an argument with Christine.'

'Oh.'

'You know I said she and I would see to milking while you all went to t'Show?'

'Aye.'

'Her Dad turned up this morning. Invited us to t'Show and to dinner, she says.'

'Turned up?' Matt exclaimed. 'Where?'

'At Hawthorn. While I was at Emmerdale.'

'Didn't he stop to see you?'

'No, she says he had an appointment.'

'Well by gum . . !'

'She says he really had. Seems like it's right, because why would he invite us to dinner if he was still avoiding me?'

'Oh yes, that's true. What have you decided to do?'

'How d'you mean, what have I decided?'

'About going to t'Show?'

'I said I'd be here to do milking,' Joe said with sudden sharpness. 'And that's that.'

'But if Mr Sharp—'

'He can invite us some other time,' Joe said. 'Do I have to run round in circles just because he's invited us to dinner?'

'Yes, but Joe—'

Joe sighed. 'The fact is, we got at cross purposes and I felt I had to put my foot down.'

'I see.'

'Nay, you don't, Matt. You've never lost your temper with anybody, I'll bet. But it's done now, and she's telephoning her dad to say we can't go. And that's that.'

Christine was at Emmerdale to do the milking that afternoon. She and Annie did it, while the men worked on the fields at Gimbels. If Annie thought she was silent, she put it down to the aftermath of last night's episode, and said nothing.

The day of the sheep trials at the Yorkshire Show came at last. Matt had gone on the previous day with his ewes, so as to groom them to perfection in the morning. The Emmerdale party, plus Henry, went off with a big picnic lunch. They sought out Matt at once and found him busy but calm. Henry knew better than to offer his inexpert help, but Sam was sure he could do better than Matt and was put out when his daughter gently led him away.

'Let be,' she told him. 'Matt knows what he's about.'

'I were handling sheep before he were born—!'

'But you haven't handled *these* sheep. He doesn't want them fussed just before they go in the ring, Dad.'

Luckily at that moment Sam was clapped on the shoulder by an old acquaintance who had moved from Emmerdale some fifteen years ago. Invited to review old times in the refreshment tent, Sam accepted with alacrity. That was how Sam managed to miss the award of the prize for the Best Ewes in Show to Matthew Skilbeck of Emmerdale Farm.

But Alison Gibbons didn't miss it. She had come on purpose to see how Matt fared, and she cheered and waved her programme at the judges' decision. By good luck, Matt looked across the grass expanse of the judging ring, and saw Alison standing there, laughing with pleasure and with her programme waving over her head at his win.

Matt met her eyes. Her face changed for a moment, and then she smiled again – directly at him, not from general pleasure at the judges' decision.

He sought her out later. She had been expecting him, for she was standing at almost the same spot. 'Well done, Matt,' she said.

'Thank you.'

'I came on purpose to raise a cheer for you.'

'That was nice of you, Alison.' He sought for the right thing to do next. 'Annie's got a big picnic meal. Would you like to join us?'

'No, thank you, Matt.'

'Come and have a cup of tea, then.'

'No, I'd rather . . .'

'Please, Alison. I'd like a word with you.'

She looked at him. She hesitated, and was lost. 'All right then.'

But when they got to the refreshment tent it was crowded. They shied away from the throng and went on instead to a space near the big display of farming equipment, where there was a surprising air of quiet.

'Henry tells me you're leaving, Alison?'

'Did he? I didn't intend it for publication.'

'It isn't publication, to tell an old friend.'

'Perhaps not. Yes, I'm going.'

'Where to?'

'Jersey. My friend Louise – you remember her?'

She broke off as she remembered how Louise had brought on the crisis between herself and Matt. Matt made no reply to her query, but said instead, 'Why are you leaving, then, Alison?'

'It just seems a good idea.'

'Are you sure? Going to a new place, starting all over again?'

'It seems best.'

'Best for who?' He looked at her, saw her shadowed face with the big eyes glinting with tears, and said quietly, 'I believe you're thinking of me and Henry. It's that, isn't it? You're in a difficult position between the two of us.'

She didn't say yea or nay to that. After a moment he said, 'What if I promised not to . . . well, you know, not to expect . . .'

'You're awfully nice, Matt,' she said, in a voice she couldn't keep steady. 'No one else could make an offer like that.'

'I just think that if you stayed, and let time go by, it would all solve itself.'

'But it's the misery and embarrassment while the time is going by, you see. I think it would be easier for all of us if I were in Jersey.'

'Everything will seem sort of empty if you go away, Alison.'

'Don't you think it's going to cost me something too?' she burst out. And then, recovering herself, 'It's best. I've thought and thought, and I don't believe I've got the strength to stand up to the strain if I stay here. It isn't so very long ago, you know, Matt, that I went completely to pieces. The psychiatrist at the prison helped me put things together again, but I don't know if I can hold on to it if I have to be pulled two ways between you and Henry.'

He took her hand. 'I'm sorry. I see what you mean. Of course you have to go, if it's best for you.'

'Best for you too, Matt.'

'Nay, I won't accept that,' he said. There was a long, painful pause, and then he said with an attempt at brightness, 'Jersey isn't the other side of the world. I could come and see you, couldn't I?'

'Well . . . Yes!' she exclaimed. All at once she faced him, smiling through her tears. 'That's true, Matt! And Jersey is a perfect place for a holiday!'

He tucked her arm through his. 'Let's go and see if we can get that cup of tea now,' he said. They threaded their way back towards the refreshment tent, and he said, 'This has been a strange few months, hasn't it? Sort of sad and happy at the same time.'

'The sad and happy summer,' she said. 'With a wedding in it, and a parting.'

'But not a final parting, Alison.'

'We can still be friends, Matt.'

Annie, watching them walk together through the crowd, felt an impulse of hope. It might turn out all right after all, somehow, some time. For Matt's sake, she hoped so. But it was all in the lap of the gods.

Far removed from the excitement and activity of the Show, Emmerdale was lying quiet in the afternoon sun. Joe and Christine had come up to the farm in Christine's car. There was still a constraint between them, but at least Christine had got past the stage of not saying a word.

Joe had felt he had to make a stand over the arrangements for today. He could have brought someone else in to do the milking, but only with great difficulty and some expense. 'Your dad has a farm,' he'd said to his wife, 'he'll understand that the milking has to be done.'

'But why do we have to stop behind to do it?'

'Because I said we would. And your dad can invite us for another day.'

Christine told him later that she had rung her father but no future date had been set for the dinner. 'He's busy,' she said shortly when he queried her on that.

'Well, so am I,' Joe agreed. He felt afterwards that the remark hadn't helped the situation.

Now they were in the kitchen at Emmerdale, the old familiar home of his childhood. He still felt he fitted into it more comfortably than into the new, bright place at Hawthorn.

'Shall we have a cup of tea before we start?' he suggested. 'We've got time.'

'If you like.'

He put the kettle on and picked up the old brown teapot. 'I wonder how Matt's doing with his ewes,' he murmured.

'He'll do well. They were in peak condition.'

'Aye, he's got a special touch wi' sheep. By and by we'll get a name for sheep breeding at Emmerdale. If I can get the milk herd accredited, we'll happen get a name for that too. Might come alongside your father's show place one day,' he ended cheerfully.

'It might pay you to be friends with him, that's a fact,' she remarked.

Joe stiffened. But he didn't want another quarrel. 'I want to be friends with him,' he said. 'You know that.'

'A funny way to show it, refusing his invitation. Considering how important he's going to be to us, it wasn't very tactful.'

'Listen, Chrissie, everybody has trouble shaking down with in-laws. I'm not going to have problems with your father if I can help it – I'll be as nice as pie to him, I promise.'

'He's done his part, at any rate.'

'By turning up unexpected at Hawthorn and issuing one invitation?'

'Oh, I didn't mean that, and you ought to know it if you'd any sense. He's done a lot for us—'

'Done a lot for us?' The kettle began to boil. Joe took it off and set it aside; teamaking was the last thing on his mind now. 'He's done damn all!'

'Oh, come *on*, Joe.'

'Tell me one thing!'

'We'd never have been able to have such a good start without him—'

'Start?'

'You don't think we could have such a nice home without—'

'Christine!' He came up to her and took her by the shoulders. 'What are you saying? How did your father help us? What do you mean?'

'But I told you! The things I bought – they went on account. I *told* you that.'

'Told me?' He delved into his mind. 'I asked you how we were going to pay for them and you said you'd opened an account.'

'No, I said I'd put them on our account.'

'Our account. Yours and mine.'

'That would have been silly, Joe. Opening a new account – when we've had one at the big shops in Leeds and Harrogate for years.'

'We?' He tightened his grip on her. 'You mean your father?'

'Joe, you're hurting me!'

He made a big effort and let her go. He was beginning to feel a red haze of anger welling up within him.

'Let's be plain,' he said. 'Let's have it out in words of one syllable. You charged the things you bought for our home – to your father's account?'

'But I thought you understood that—'

'Wait, Christine. The wedding reception? You said they'd send a bill for that. Who is the bill going to?'

'My father, of course. The father of the bride always pays for the reception.'

'But . . . Christine . . . you told me you had broken off with your father completely.'

'But that was *before*. Parents always come round after the wedding. I knew Daddy would soften.'

'So you arranged for the bill from the caterer to go to him? And – wait a minute – the bill for having the floor sanded and polished? And the Persian rugs? And the antique chairs?'

'But why do you say it like that? It's all in the family, Joe—'

'In *your* family,' he said. 'You told me, when we discussed it once, that you had some money in the bank.'

'Yes, that's right.'

'I thought that was to be spent on the furniture, as far as it would go. And that after that, I would pay for it by and by.'

'Oh, let's talk sense, Joe. You just couldn't ever have met the bills. And I spent my own money on the wedding dress and things like that – going away clothes, new luggage . . .'

'My God.' He said it in a low voice. He felt as if he had had a kick in the pit of his stomach.

'I don't see why you're making a big thing of it,' Christine protested, looking bewildered and alarmed. 'What does it matter who pays? Daddy's got plenty of money—'

'And does he by any chance imagine that I go along with this idea, that he should pay for setting up my home?'

'He's not bothered. It's my home too, after all.'

'*Christine!* He disapproved of the marriage so completely that he wouldn't answer any of my letters and wouldn't come to the wedding.'

'Mummy came,' she reminded him.

'Yes – came, and went. Happen she'd have stayed longer if she'd known she was paying for it.' He looked grim. 'Did she know that everything was being charged to your father?'

'Mummy couldn't care less. She and Daddy don't see each other much. Anyhow, it's more important to be on friendly terms with Daddy.'

'Oh yes, I can see that. There's no way we're going to live up to the standard you expect if we don't cadge off him.'

'Joe!' she cried. 'It isn't cadging. I mean, it's only money – and Daddy's got plenty. What does it matter who pays?'

'It matters to me,' he replied. 'I thought you'd have understood that.' He walked to the window and stared out, unseeing, at the sunlight on the old trees by the path. 'How much does it come to?'

'What?'

'All this that you've spent – the wedding, the furniture, everything. How much?'

'Oh, *I* don't know, Joe!'

'But you must have some idea?'

'No, I haven't, because the bills have gone to Daddy's address.'

'Dear God,' Joe muttered. 'And I was to go and have dinner with him, without ever knowing I owed him a lot of money?'

'But you don't owe anything,' she insisted. 'Daddy doesn't expect you to pay it.'

'If it's the last thing I do, I'll settle those bills,' he said in a low tone. 'So how much is it?'

'I tell you I don't know!'

'The reception – you must have had an estimate for that?'

'I didn't bother. We'd used the firm before—'

'I see. What sort of cost would it be? A hundred?'

She laughed in surprise.

'More? Two hundred?'

'Well . . . I suppose . . . perhaps.'

'Two hundred. How much for the furniture? The reproduction table, those damned antique armchairs?'

'I forget—'

'Tell me, Christine. You must have seen a price tag on them when you bought them.'

'I tell you I forget. I think the table was . . . I think it was two-eighty.'

'Two hundred and eighty pounds?' Joe echoed, aghast.

'It's a very good reproduction!'

'So the chairs, then . . .' He drew himself up. He could picture the chairs, and he suddenly knew they were very costly. 'Are they about the same price.'

'I think I paid three hundred for them.'

'The pair?'

'No, six hundred the pair.'

Joe leaned against the draining board, half closing his eyes. They had topped a thousand pounds already, and they had by no means finished. There was the elegant china she had insisted on buying, the curtains, the Persian rugs . . .

'I'll ask your father to give me a total,' he said.

'Don't you dare!' she flashed. 'That's only going to cause an unpleasantness. Of course Daddy expects to pay to see me properly set up in my new home.'

'You mean a man who disapproves of his daughter's marriage is supposed to pay through the nose to set her up?'

'What's all the fuss about?' she said, a note of genuine irritation coming into her voice. 'It's so . . . so small-minded to keep on about money like this.'

'I've had to be small-minded about it all my life,' he returned, his face hardening at the word. 'I thought you understood that. We don't have that kind of money. And I don't intend to run my married life with somebody else's.'

'But you've no choice, Joe. Don't be pig-headed. You can't ever pay for the things I've bought so why don't you just let it go?'

'Is that what you thought when you went shopping? Joe can never pay for them but it doesn't matter, I can charge it all to Daddy and Joe can't do a thing.'

'I didn't think of it that way. You're putting words into my mouth.'

'Then tell me what was in your mind, Christine. Because from where I'm standing, it looks like downright deceit.'

'Deceit?' Her eyes glinted with anger. 'I didn't deceive you. I told you I was putting the things on account.'

'You led me to think that I would eventually be paying for them.'

'But you must have *known* you wouldn't, Joe.'

It was true. From her point of view, it must have been clear that she had bought goods far beyond his ability to pay. He had been a stupid dolt. He had never really questioned her, never put up any embargoes. He had let her run his life from the moment they got engaged, being persuaded to move into Matt's home, letting her turn out Matt's belongings, running them into debt, foisting her ideas on him at every turn. He had made no objection. He was a fool, a ninny, a blockhead, a weakling.

And the realization only made him the more angry and desperate. He said, 'Did you think we could keep on like that? The dinner you put on for Ma and everybody – did you buy those things at a shop where your family has an account?'

'Well . . .'

'By Christ,' he said, 'I think your father was right after all in what he said. You do live in a fantasy world.'

'My father?' Christine, sitting at the kitchen table, suddenly turned in her chair to stare at him. 'You've never met my father.'

'I've met him. We ran across each other by mere accident at Loudwick Market.'

'You've . . . met him?'

'It were just before we were married.'

'You didn't tell me!'

'No.' He had never been able to bring himself to mention that strange encounter to her, because to do so might mean telling her Mr Sharp's harsh advice – 'Break it off while you still have time.'

'You kept it from me!' she cried. Her voice was odd, cracking with stress.

'It seemed best at the time,' he said. 'I couldn't make head nor tail of his attitude.'

'But you understand it now,' she flashed. 'You listened to the rotten things he said about me and now you throw them in my face.'

'I'm not going to go over all that,' Joe said, shaking his head. 'It's what we have to deal with *now* that matters.'

'You discussed me with him. You did, didn't you?'

'Naturally we talked about you, Christine. What else would we talk about?'

'And you didn't tell me. You lied to me,' she said, and her voice had fallen to a strange whisper, 'you lied to me!'

'No, I didn't. I just thought it best not to mention—'

'You lied to me!'

She sprang up and ran out, leaving the door wide open. He was so taken aback that for a moment he didn't pull himself together to follow her. By the time he got to the door she was throwing herself into the little white sports car.

'Christine!' he shouted.

She started the engine and began to turn the car. He ran towards it, but she paid no heed. She only just missed him as she went on a curve out of the farmyard. The car door was still swinging open.

'Christine!'

But the car was already in the lane, heading away from him at breakneck speed. He stood helpless while it raced on, taking Christine away from him.

For a minute or more he listened to the sound of the engine fading away on the quiet afternoon air. He could tell she had taken the turn for Leeds, that she had not headed for Hawthorn Cottage.

By and by he became aware that the cows had moved into their line for the milking parlour. He could hear the movements, the occasional lowing of expectation. He glanced at his watch; it was time to get started. Whatever else might happen in his life, the animals couldn't be neglected.

He worked alone, methodically, keeping his mind on what he was doing. When he had finished the milking and the washing down he made sure the feed was measured in, and tidied up the sack of nuts. It took him longer than if he had had help.

He had just finished when the Landrover came into the yard with Matt at the wheel, and behind it Henry's car with his mother and grandfather. Annie got out, nodded at Joe, and went into the kitchen. The rest followed her, aglow with happiness at the result of the day at the Show.

Joe wanted above all to make his escape before his mother became aware of what had happened. He would have been gone, except that he couldn't find his jacket. He still hadn't discovered where he had put it when he heard her voice calling to him.

'Joe! Joe, you there?'

There was no help for it. 'Yes, I'm here, Ma.'

'Thought you must be. Your jacket's still in t'kitchen.' She came to the door of the milking parlour. 'Staying for tea?'

'Nay, I don't think I will, thanks, Ma.'

'Oh, why don't you? You want to hear about Matt and the sheep, don't you?' She paused. It occurred to her that it was strange he hadn't asked. 'Matt won,' she said.

'Oh, that's great. I'm very pleased, Ma. Tell him congratulations.'

She came inside, into the dimmer light of the mistle. 'Is anything wrong, Joe?'

'No, everything's fine, Ma. Fine.'

But she was not deceived. 'Where's Christine?'

He came towards her. They were only a few inches apart.

'She's gone, Ma.'

'Gone?' Although his tone told a lot, she clutched at some slight hope. 'To see her father after all?'

Joe shook his head. 'No, I think she's gone for good. Left me.'

'Nay . . . son . . . you've had a quarrel. She'll be back.'

He shook his head. 'I don't think so, Ma. I think the marriage is over. In fact,' – and his voice was weary – 'I don't think it ever began.'

Annie put a hand on his shoulder. 'You go home,' she said. 'I'll tell t'others you and Christine have plans for the evening. Happen she'll be back later.'

He obeyed, turning to the door. His mother saw the sag of the young shoulders, and knew it was serious – he meant it when he said he thought his marriage was over.

She watched him go. He walked quickly, but without his usual vigour. 'Ah, lad, lad,' Annie said within herself, 'thou'st had a blow, I wish I could have taken it for thee . . .'

With a deep breath to steady herself she went back indoors, to prepare a meal for the menfolk. She would say nothing for the present. Time enough to let them know if and when anything more came of it.

She had no real idea what the quarrel had been about. She could only tell that it would have repercussions over many months. But whatever happened, she would keep Emmerdale as it had always been – a home to which Joe could return without fear of reproach.

GENERAL FICTION

0352 Star

	Michael J. Bird	
301481	**WHO PAYS THE FERRYMAN?**	85p ◆
	William Burroughs	
39613X	**DEAD FINGERS TALK**	75p
	Jackie Collins	
395621	**THE STUD**	65p
300701	**LOVEHEAD**	70p
398663	**THE WORLD IS FULL OF DIVORCED WOMEN**	50p
398752	**THE WORLD IS FULL OF MARRIED MEN**	50p
	Robertson Davies	
396113	**FIFTH BUSINESS**	95p
	Alexander Edwards	
396881	**A STAR IS BORN**	60p ◆
	Robert Grossbach	
30166X	**THE GOODBYE GIRL**	60p* ◆
	W. Harris	
301406	**SALIVA**	70p
	Dan Jenkins	
302100	**SEMI-TOUGH**	75p* ◆
	Jeffrey Konvitz	
398981	**THE SENTINEL**	70p* ◆
	Dean R. Koontz	
301643	**NIGHT CHILLS**	75p*
	Lee Mackenzie	
396903	**EMMERDALE FARM (No. 1) THE LEGACY**	50p ◆
396298	**EMMERDALE FARM (No. 2) PRODIGAL'S PROGRESS**	60p ◆
395974	**EMMERDALE FARM (No. 3) ALL THAT A MAN HAS . . .**	60p ◆
301414	**EMMERDALE FARM (No. 4) LOVERS' MEETING**	60p ◆
301422	**EMMERDALE FARM (No. 5) A SAD AND HAPPY SUMMER**	60p ◆
	Graham Masterton	
396164	**THE MANITOU**	70p ◆
39526 5	**THE DJINN**	75p*

† For sale in Britain and Ireland only.
*Not for sale in Canada.
◆ Film & T.V. tie-ins.

GENERAL FICTION

0352	397403	Robert Stone **DOG SOLDIERS**	75p*
	395427	Peter Upton **GREEN HILL FAR AWAY**	95p
	301570	Margaret Walker **JUBILEE**	95p*
	301562	N. Richard Nash **EAST WIND, RAIN**	95p*
	395540	Gail Parent **DAVID MEYER IS A MOTHER**	70p
	300809	Molly Parkin **LOVE ALL**	50p
	397179	**UP TIGHT**	60p
	396288	Erich Maria Remarque **BOBBY DEERFIELD**	85p* ♦
	396946	Judith Rossner **TO THE PRECIPICE**	85p*
	302089	**NINE MONTHS IN THE LIFE OF AN OLD MAID**	75p*
	398892	Alan Sillitoe **THE GENERAL**	50p
	300965	**THE LONELINESS OF THE LONG-DISTANCE RUNNER**	50p
	300949	**MEN, WOMEN AND CHILDREN**	50p
	300981	**SATURDAY NIGHT AND SUNDAY MORNING**	50p
	395141	**THE WIDOWER'S SON**	85p
	397144	**THE FLAME OF LIFE**	70p
	398809	**THE RAGMAN'S DAUGHTER**	50p
	396415	Hubert Selby Jr. **THE ROOM**	75p

† For sale in Britain and Ireland only.
*Not for sale in Canada.
♦ Film & T.V. tie-ins.